Best Wishes,
Linda W. Clarke

MELINDA AND
THE WILD WEST

A Family Saga in
Bear Lake Valley, Idaho

By
Linda Weaver Clarke

Bedside Books
An imprint of American Book Publishing
P.O. Box 65624
Salt Lake City, UT 84165
www.american-book.com
Printed in the United States of America on acid-free paper.

Melinda and the Wild West

Designed by George Amos Clarke, design@american-book.com

Publisher's Note: This is a work of fiction. Names, characters, places, and incidents either are the product of the author's imagination, or are used fictitiously, and any resemblance to actual persons, living or dead, events, or locales is entirely coincidental.

ISBN 1-58982-367-2

Clarke, Linda Weaver, Melinda and the Wild West

Special Sales

These books are available at special discounts for bulk purchases. Special editions, including personalized covers, excerpts of existing books, and corporate imprints, can be created in large quantities for special needs. For more information e-mail info@american-book.com.

MELINDA AND THE WILD WEST

A Family Saga in
Bear Lake Valley, Idaho

By
Linda Weaver Clarke

To the memory of
Gilbert and Sarah Weaver
(1835–1909)
My great-great-grandparents:
the first pioneers who settled
Paris, Idaho

Chapter 1
HEADING WEST

The steel wheels of the train roared as they sped down the tracks. Looking out the window of the train, Melinda was in awe as she eyed the majestic Rocky Mountains before her. The jagged cliffs were magnificent and she could not take her eyes off the inspiring view. The flat, rich meadowland spread out for miles and miles between the mountains, exhibiting more shades of green and yellow than she could ever have imagined; and among all this were patches of bright red Indian paintbrush that seemed to set the land on fire. She had never seen such splendid scenery in her life, and certainly not something as grand as this. She was used to the city life with all its hustle and bustle, the street noises, the towering buildings, and the rolling hills.

Melinda noticed a deer gracefully sprinting across the field as if it were flying in midair. A hawk lazily glided through the air, searching the ground for a meal. At every bend, a romantic scene opened before her. The serenity and peace that she felt here were new to her.

Melinda was heading west. As she looked out the window at the passing scenery, she suddenly remembered Boston, her home, and the day that would change her life forever. She had received a very special letter in the mail from her father's oldest sister, Aunt Martha, who lived out west in southern Idaho. It had been about twelve years since she had seen her favorite aunt. The last time she had seen Martha, Melinda had been only fourteen years old. They kept in contact through letters, though, and now Melinda was twenty-six, a graduate from college, and still unmarried.

Melinda pulled a letter out of her golden-flowered carpetbag and unfolded it. She smoothed it against her lap and reread it with excitement in her heart.

> *My dearest Melinda,*
>
> *How I've missed you! I have very exciting news for you. A teaching position has opened up out here in Paris, Idaho, and they are looking for a teacher. Will you please consider this position? You could stay with us. We have plenty of room since my last child left home for college. I am looking forward to a quick reply. Love, Aunt Martha*

Out west! Melinda had never been out west before. The invitation was so enticing. She had heard stories of the West, seen pictures of the scenery in books, and deep inside herself she longed to see it up close and be a part of it.

Her mother, after hearing about the letter, was not too happy. "Melinda, you have a life here. How about James? I know that he wants to marry you."

"But Mama, I'm not in love with him, and he knows it, too."

"Melinda, that comes with time. It comes with marriage. Don't expect to be swept off your feet, my dear."

Melinda pressed her hand to her heart as she said, "Mama, that's what I want! To be swept off my feet, to have my heart flutter at the sight of him. That's what I want and it doesn't happen when I'm with James."

"But that only happens in fairy tales, sweetheart. Are you waiting for a knight in shining armor to save you from a ferocious beast and take you into his arms and ride off together on his white horse? You are now twenty-six years of age and it's about time you settled down and stopped daydreaming about something that won't ever happen. Be sensible. You are far too particular. James is a wonderful man and he loves you. I don't understand what you're waiting for."

"Mama, it's 1896." Melinda said as she slammed her hand down upon the dining room table. "Women can make choices about their own lives more than ever before. I chose to go to college even though women aren't encouraged to do so, and that choice made all the difference in the world. I'm a different person now just because of that choice. I know what I want in life and I know James isn't the one. I want to go west. I don't want to stay here." Melinda had a determined tone in her voice and her mother responded to it with concern.

3

"But the West is too wild. I've read about the things that happen out there. There are dangerous outlaws, wild Indians, unruly cowboys, and uncouth ranchers. They don't know how to treat a lady."

"Mama, I can handle the West. Don't worry about me."

Her mother shook her head in despair, knowing that her daughter had already made up her mind. "Melinda, I can see that you're determined to do this and I know that I can say nothing to change your mind because you are so self-willed. When you get an idea in your head, you won't stop and consider whether it's right or not."

Melinda instantly bolted to her feet, her face creased with a look of displeasure. "Self-willed?" Melinda's voice was laced with impatience. "I just hate it when you tell me that I'm self-willed, Mama. The fact is, I know what I want." Melinda was exasperated. She hated that phrase and would have stormed out of the room if it were not for the respect she had for her mother.

With a calm voice, her mother said, "But you *are* self-willed, Melinda. You've been like that ever since you were a child."

Melinda took a deep breath and let it out slowly, then looked into her mother's eyes. "Mama, I'm not self-willed. I'm determined. I know that there is a life out there for me. I feel it inside my heart. And my heart tells me to go."

Melinda's mother rose from her seat and took Melinda's hand in hers. Softly, she said, "I don't know why you've been so restless lately. What do you want in life?"

"I want to do some good in the world, and perhaps make a difference in someone's life. Maybe I can do some good in the West by teaching school."

To make a difference—that was it, she thought as she saw a small town appear ahead of her. Melinda had a desire to do some good and help others, to bring knowledge to the innocent minds of young children. Maybe teaching school in the West was what she needed.

The train began to slow down and she could see the terminal up ahead. With the arrival of the railroad in 1892, the town of Montpelier had become the home terminal for the Union Pacific/Oregon Short Line Trains. Peering out the window, she searched for her aunt and uncle as the train came to a screeching stop.

Melinda picked up her carpetbag and carefully walked down the steps of the train, holding her skirts up so she would not step on them. As she stepped down to the ground, the attendants and men at the terminal stared. It had been a long time since they had seen a lady like her come into town. Melinda was a strikingly beautiful woman with eyes as green as emeralds. She was an unusually tall and slender woman. Because of her height, many heads turned and Melinda found herself the object of conversation, which embarrassed and annoyed her quite a bit. People seemed to notice her simply because she was tall. Why not because she was intelligent or had a charming personality?

Melinda wiped a stray curl from her brow and nervously smoothed a few wrinkles from her dress with her hand. She was dressed in a violet muslin dress that was gathered at the shoulder with puffed sleeves to the elbow and a lace collar. To add to the elegance of this dress, it was gathered at the waist and she had plenty of petticoats beneath to give body to her skirts, which accentuated the slimness of her figure. Her creamy skin and slender throat were emphasized by her dark auburn hair, which was loosely piled upon her head with three tortoise-shell combs holding it in place.

Looking around, she felt lost. "Where are they?" she murmured aloud.

Melinda felt uncomfortable as she noticed that she was the object of conversation among the passersby and the men who worked at the terminal. She felt ill at ease as she searched the ramp for her relatives.

"Who are you looking for, ma'am?" the train attendant asked as he placed her trunk beside her.

"My aunt and uncle. They were going to meet me here."

"Melinda!" Her aunt's voice rang from the far end of the terminal. Aunt Martha began to run toward her and they met with outspread arms.

Uncle William followed slowly behind with a friendly smile as he watched the two women embrace. He was a short, round, heavy man with a salt-and-pepper mustache and thin graying hair. He was a jovial fellow and was loved by all. Aunt Martha was a slender woman and was as tall as her husband, about medium height. Her hair was gray and placed upon her head in a loose bun and she had a twinkle in her eyes.

After hugging one another, Aunt Martha asked, "Is this all of your luggage?"

"No, the attendant is coming with two more trunks."

"Two more?" Uncle William gasped. "Sure hope they fit in our little carriage."

After loading the three trunks, they headed down the street for home. Aunt Martha smiled as she put an arm around Melinda's shoulders. "Melinda, it is so nice to see you. You have really grown since I last saw you. And you are so beautiful. I just knew you would be, even after seeing you at fourteen years old. You just had to be. My, the young men here enjoy dancing and I know that you will not be sitting on the sidelines at the dance socials, that's certain."

Melinda blushed. She felt embarrassed when family members would talk about her looks and discuss it in front of her. She wished they would not discuss it. It made her feel self-conscious and uncomfortable.

"The train terminal is in Montpelier, but we live in a little community called Paris, just ten miles south from here. That's where you'll teach." Martha waved toward the mountains with widened eyes and excitement as she continued. "This little valley is located in the tops of the Rocky Mountains. It's quite lovely, set comfortably between these mountains with a large lake nearby called Bear Lake, which is located ten miles south of Paris."

"Bear Lake?"

"Yes." Excitement seemed to fill every fiber of her being, simply because her beloved niece was finally here, a dream she had long awaited. "It's named after the bears that roam around here. The mountain men came to this area around 1818 for trapping and hunting. Fats McKenzie attended one of the Indian gatherings at the south end of Bear Lake in 1819 and named it 'Black Bear Lake' because black bears were abundant in the area. But we've just shortened it to 'Bear Lake.' It's seven-and-a-half miles wide and twenty miles long. Also, we have something that other lakes don't have and that's the Bonneville Cisco fish.

They're indigenous to this area. No other lake has this kind of fish that I know of."

As the carriage sped along the road, Melinda held her hand against her hair, keeping it in place as the warm breezes swept across her face. She turned to her aunt and asked, "Did you say the Bonneville Cisco?"

"Yes, they're quite small fish. You need to catch a lot for a satisfying meal. I'll take you for a ride to see it after you've settled down."

Uncle William gave Martha a sidelong glance and chuckled jovially. "Martha, I think that if you give Melinda any more Bear Lake history, her mind will be swimming. I suggest that you tell her a little at a time each day so she can remember it."

Martha leaned against William's shoulder and squeezed his arm lovingly. "Anything you say, dear."

After traveling over a dusty and bumpy road, they arrived at their home in Paris, next to the West Mountains. Uncle William took the trunks out of the carriage and put them in the spare bedroom upstairs while Aunt Martha showed Melinda around the house.

Martha's house was a comfortable and charming home. The living room had an attractive fireplace with a sofa and four soft chairs placed evenly around the fireplace, and a piano was set on the opposite end of the room. Straight ahead from the outside door was a white-framed door that led into a large roomy kitchen with a table and six chairs. From the living room on the right side was a staircase with a white railing that led up to the bedrooms. As Melinda ascended the stairs, she noticed pictures of family members hanging on the wall of the staircase that were placed evenly apart. She realized that her aunt was meticulous in all that she did.

After Melinda freshened up, she put on a simple pink-flowered muslin dress and Aunt Martha took her to the tiny one-room schoolhouse that was located in the center of town. It was a quaint, wood-framed schoolhouse and she noticed that it had a fresh coat of white paint.

Melinda reverently walked up the steps of the school-house and opened the door. When she entered, the floor squeaked under her feet. She looked around and saw that the desks were lined up evenly in four rows with five desks in each row. The wooden desks each had a hole in the upper right hand corner for a glass inkwell. Right away, Melinda thought she would have to assign someone the job of "inkwell monitor." This person would keep the inkwells filled. As she looked at the floor, she saw a few large blue stains on the wood floor where some of the ink had spilled. She realized that she would have to get someone with steady hands to fill the wells.

The books were piled in neat stacks on the bookshelf. Melinda took the books down to check them one at a time and found a book on Bear Lake Valley. She thumbed through it and decided to take it home with her. If she was going to be a part of this valley, then she needed to know more about it. Also, she thought it would be good to teach the children some of their own history along with that of the entire world.

But Melinda's true love was music, and she decided that these children would have plenty of that. She had majored in music at the university and had been teaching children piano and singing lessons in Boston ever since. Melinda had a beautiful rich alto voice. Many had told her that she had a pleasing and soothing voice and that always made her very happy. Singing brought her great pleasure and it pleased her when she could bring that same joy to others.

Putting the rest of the books back, she tucked the book about Bear Lake Valley under her arm and met Aunt Martha at the door. She could tell her aunt had been watching her by the expression of unbridled enthusiasm on her face.

"Aunt Martha, could you see if someone could donate a piano for the school? I would like to teach music to the children also."

Aunt Martha nodded with a smile.

Next, Martha decided to show Melinda their magnificent lake. As they rode toward it, Melinda eyed the valley that extended for miles and miles before her. They passed acres of farmland and pastureland, and she saw hundreds of cattle that were grazing in fenced pastures. She noticed that, since Paris was nestled in the tops of the Rocky Mountains, they seemed more like rolling hills than mountains.

When they came upon the lake, her eyes widened at its beautiful aqua color. It was not the color of the blue sky, but the most beautiful pristine aqua color that she had ever seen in her life and it shimmered as the sun sparkled upon it.

In the distance, Melinda could hear what sounded like hundreds of squawking birds. At the north end of Bear Lake, seventeen acres of marshland, grasslands, and open water was the home of these lovely birds during the summer months. What a splendid sight! There were Canada geese, ducks of all kinds, and ibis, sandhill cranes, and pelicans. The birds seemed to be singing in their own little choir. It was a glorious spectacle, and peacefulness over-took her as she listened to the waves softly lapping against the shoreline.

Melinda realized that she would need to explore this val-ley with short walks each day. This was now her new home.

Chapter 2
THE BANK ROBBERY

The following day, Melinda sat at the table enjoying lunch and a pleasant conversation with her aunt and uncle. As she took a bite of overdone, dried roast beef, she asked, "Why is it so hard to cook roast beef and make it have a moist and tasty flavor? I have never in my life tasted a well-seasoned roast."

Aunt Martha laughed softly, "Don't worry, my dear. You'll catch on to it some day. Some people just have a knack for cooking. It's the same with me. Some days it's moist and other days it's dry, and I can never figure out the secret."

Melinda turned to her uncle and asked, "Uncle William, may I please take the carriage into Montpelier? I have some errands to run. School starts in a couple of weeks and I need to order some supplies and open my own account at the bank. I want to save enough money to get my own place in the future."

Aunt Martha smiled. "It sounds like you plan to stay here for a while. I'm so glad because I miss having family around."

Melinda stood and as she walked toward the kitchen door, she looked over her shoulder and said, "I haven't made up my mind yet, Aunt Martha. But one needs to save for the future, no matter what."

Melinda put on a lovely white muslin dress that was fitted snugly to the bodice and gathered at the waist. It had puffed sleeves at the elbow and hung smoothly and gracefully, hugging her hips. She placed a white flower on the side of her dark tresses that were loosely pulled into an attractive bun with a few loose curls at the nape of her neck. Smiling at herself in the mirror, she pinched her cheeks for color. Grabbing her handbag, she gracefully glided down the stairs.

Melinda climbed carefully into the carriage, holding her skirts up. After she settled down, Uncle William handed her the reins to the horse. "He's gentle. You won't have any problem. Just remember to hold on tight so you have control at all times."

"All right, Uncle William. Thank you."

Realizing the time, Melinda whipped the reins and sped down the road toward Montpelier. When she arrived in town, she placed her order for school supplies and then headed toward the bank to deposit the last of her money. It was August thirteenth; school would begin in only two weeks and she had a long list of chores to accomplish before then.

Approaching the bank, she noticed a sign next to the door that said "The Bank of Montpelier, Established in

1891." Looking at her watch, Melinda realized she had arrived just in time, before the bank closed.

The bank president and his friend were visiting on the steps of the bank. When Melinda approached, they cordially greeted her as they tipped their hats and smiled, "Good day, ma'am."

Melinda smiled back as she opened the door of the bank. Inside, she asked the teller for papers to open an account. As she was filling out the papers, she heard the door slowly squeak open and shut. Melinda glanced up and saw four men enter the bank with very sober faces: the two gentlemen who were on the steps and two other men who were dressed like cowhands or cowboys. As they entered, she noticed that one of the cowboys mumbled something to the men in front of him who quickly stiffened with fear in their eyes. Melinda looked questioningly at them, wondering what was wrong. Then one of the cowboys closed the door, and as they backed away from the gentlemen, she realized they had guns in their hands.

Melinda gasped, dropping her pen to the floor. Her heart began to throb and her face paled as she realized she was witnessing, firsthand, the reason this place was called the "Wild West." As she watched, her eyes brimmed with anxious tears and her chest tightened.

"Up against the wall," the outlaw demanded.

Melinda looked around and the only other people in the bank were a woman stenographer and a male teller by the name of Mackintosh.

Melinda was so frightened that her breathing became short and irregular. Her eyes widened with the terror of not knowing what would happen next. She had read stories about Butch Cassidy and the Wild Bunch and she remembered an outlaw by the name of Kid Curry who was known as the most feared killer in the West, and the memory of it sent chills down her spine. Kid Curry was one of the Wild Bunch.

"Well, well, Cassidy," the outlaw drawled. "Look what we have here. Two women, and one purtier than I've ever seen before."

The outlaw's eyes boldly swept over Melinda's body, from her hair down to her shoes with a look that sent a chill up her spine. His look greatly offended her and she knew the fear she felt was obvious to everyone. Cassidy saw the troubled look on Melinda's face and he quickly intervened.

"Elza, don't frighten her. She's a lady. Look at her dress and the way she holds herself. I saw ladies like her when I went back East last year."

Cassidy took off his hat and flashed her a gentle smile. It seemed to her that he had great respect for women. Aunt Martha had told her that most cowboys did. If any cowboy or outlaw showed disrespect to a woman, or treated her inappropriately, his peers soon corrected him for his behavior. Melinda noticed that even though Cassidy did not respect the law, he deeply respected a lady.

Cassidy gave her a charming smile and said softly, "Ma'am, don't be frightened. I can see you are, but we won't hurt you. I promise."

Melinda stared at him for the longest time. His voice was kind and his eyes were soft; his manner seemed to contradict everything he represented. He was a handsome man with a boyish look in his face. His hair was short with bangs parted to the side. Butch Cassidy was known for his

16

charm and quick wit, not to mention his fearlessness and bravery. He had an air of authority about him and no one could mistake that he was the leader of his gang.

Mr. Gray, the bank president, exclaimed with surprise, "Did you say Cassidy? As in Butch Cassidy, the outlaw?"

Cassidy grinned and nodded with a sparkle of mischief in his eyes as he put his hat back on. "Heard of me?"

Gray tried not to stammer, but it was impossible. "Uh...y-yes, I have. D-don't they call your gang the Wild Bunch?"

"They sure do," he said with pride in his voice. With a command of authority, he looked at everyone. "Now all of you, against the wall so we can do our job."

Melinda was standing at the teller's window, and as Cassidy momentarily turned his attention to the two gentlemen in the corner, Mackintosh leaned over and whispered, "I heard that Cassidy was born in Utah, and was raised by kind and religious parents. When he was a teenager, he fell under the influence of an old rustler and soon left home to ride the outlaw trail, taking on the name of his mentor."

Upon hearing this, Melinda realized that others had influenced Cassidy, encouraging him to disregard his parents' teachings. He could have been an asset to the community but had chosen another direction. How many other children had gone astray simply because of being swayed by friends?

Elza Lay was a part of Cassidy's gang, as well as his best friend. Lay was a tall, slender, handsome man known for being a top bronco rider and ranch hand. He was a flirtatious sort of fellow and seemed to have a way with women and horses.

Elza could not take his eyes off Melinda as he boldly scanned every inch of her. His penetrating glare unnerved her and she quickly averted her eyes. As his eyes studied her, he commanded, "Give me your purse."

Melinda clutched her purse tightly with both hands. It was the last of her money. The protest inside her wedged in her throat and she could not speak. Her chest tightened until she could scarcely breathe.

Seeing her panic, Cassidy intervened once again. "Leave her alone, Elza. We have all we need here at the bank." Turning to the hostages, he demanded, "Now the rest of you, turn around with your faces toward the wall."

Elza Lay leaned casually against the writing desk with his revolver pointed at his hostages while Cassidy quickly scooped up the money into a gunnysack.

Lay's eyes were steady upon Melinda and she became very uncomfortable. "Hurry, Cassidy. Meeks is holding the horses. You know how nervous he gets."

Melinda looked out the window and noticed the third man standing by the horses across the street. She made a mental note of the man's features just before Lay struck Mackintosh across the face.

"Where's the rest of the money?" Lay demanded.

Losing his balance, Mackintosh bumped into Melinda. She took his arm to steady him and asked in a quiet tone, "Are you all right?"

He nodded somewhat unconvincingly, his eyes wide with fear.

"Well, where is the rest of it?" Lay demanded as he stared at Mackintosh.

"Uh...th-that's all. Th-there's no more. We only took in about $7,000."

Cassidy shoved the last of the money in the sack. "You know, Elza, I figur'd the best way to hurt 'em is through their pocketbook. I can assure you they will holler louder than if you cut off both legs. In fact, I like to steal their money just to hear 'em holler. Then, just like Robin Hood, I pass it out among those who really need it, taking from the rich and giving to the poor."

Melinda remembered hearing how he proclaimed that he was fighting for the settlers' rights against the rich cattle baron. To some he was a hero but to Melinda and other law-abiding citizens, he was a bandit.

Cassidy walked to the door and stopped. Looking at Melinda, he gave her a charming smile and nodded. "Ma'am, I'm sorry if we frightened you."

Cassidy held the gunnysack in a casual manner and slowly left the bank. He walked nonchalantly across the street as if he did not have a care in the world. He fastened the gunnysack to his saddlebags and then swung himself upon his horse and rode slowly away. No one seemed to take notice of this stranger or suspect anything was wrong as he rode down the street, passing people on his way.

Melinda noticed that everything was planned down to the last moment. Cassidy apparently never acted without a well-staked-out plan. Watching from the window, she noticed that after Cassidy was out of town, Meeks moved across the street toward the bank with the remaining horses and left Lay's horse standing in front of the bank. Meeks hopped upon his horse and slowly rode away. Again, no one took notice of the second stranger, riding off down the road.

Through the bank window, Lay watched Meeks ride out of town. Before he left, he softly stroked Melinda's cheek with his fingers and gave her a smile that shook her nerves.

"Bye, purty lady."

Melinda's stomach was all in knots. She wanted to cry out of relief that they were gone, and yet she wanted to give that outlaw a piece of her mind for the way he had frightened everyone and for the way he had looked at her. So this was the Wild West that she had been reading about. Melinda found out how wild the West really was, and it was only her second day in town!

As soon as Elza Lay left the bank and headed down the street on his horse, it seemed as if all pandemonium erupted as Gray ran outside and alerted everyone, including the sheriff and deputy. Melinda watched from the window as Deputy Fred Cruikshank took off on his bicycle for home so he could saddle up his horse. Attorney Bagley followed after him so they could immediately take off together, while Sheriff Jefferson Davis called for a posse, which only took minutes to do.

Melinda walked outside to watch all the commotion. As they sped down the street, Melinda watched in awe as each man passed her on his horse with a revolver buckled at his hip.

Mackintosh walked up to her and looked her in the face. "You're new here, aren't you?"

She nodded and swallowed a lump in her throat before answering, "I'm the new schoolteacher in Paris."

"Well, this sure is a way to welcome a new school teacher. Are you all right? You look a bit shaken."

She nodded again as she wiped her hands nervously against her skirt. It was hard to speak. Her mouth was dry, her hands were damp, her face was ashen, and her mind was in a whirl.

"You know, ma'am, the thirteenth was the cause of it all."

Melinda stared at Macintosh and looked puzzled.

"Yes, the thirteenth. You see, today is the thirteenth day of the month; it took place after the thirteenth deposit had been made today in the amount of thirteen dollars; and the robbery transpired at thirteen minutes after three o'clock."

Chapter 3
THE RUGGED STRANGER

The following day, Melinda felt that she had now been officially introduced to the western world. Everything she had read in books about the West was coming to life before her very eyes. The funny thing about it was that she had expected an outlaw to look ugly and mean, but Cassidy did not look that way. He was, in fact, rather attractive and cordial. Melinda could not help but wonder, what makes a person go the direction that Cassidy did? Often, she knew, parents needed help from others to keep their child on the straight-and-narrow path. So if the parents needed help, where was the community to lend a hand? Where were the teachers to help instill values? This was something to think about. Melinda vowed that she would be ready: If she came upon a child who needed help, she would be there.

Upon hearing how delicious the raspberries were in the Bear Lake Valley, Melinda helped Aunt Martha pick a bunch of plump raspberries from her raspberry patch. It was the most delicious fruit she had ever tasted in her life. She could not wait to put cream and sugar on them for supper.

After picking a basketful, Melinda took a stroll along the countryside to enjoy the fresh air. She knew she would not have much spare time after school began because of the responsibilities as a teacher. It did not take long until she found a lush and beautiful field with a cool stream nearby. So, lifting her skirts, she carefully climbed the fence so she could investigate this beautiful scenery.

Melinda felt a freedom she had never felt before. As the breeze gently brushed past her cheeks, she suddenly felt an exuberant need to run. Lifting up her skirts, she ran through the field toward the stream, where she tossed aside her shoes and socks. Melinda gathered her skirts with her left hand and held them up as she walked down the middle of the stream, her right hand poised to keep her balance. The fresh, cool water trickled against her ankles and it felt so refreshing.

Melinda stopped for a moment and watched a couple of birds flying and swooping in the air, chasing one another. Is this a form of courtship or are they having a lover's spat? she wondered. The thought made her laugh out loud and her long eyelashes seemed to flirt with the breeze as she waded through the stream.

Melinda noticed the stream curved to the right. Looking up, she was startled to see someone watching her in the middle of her reverie. She stopped abruptly where she was and her lips parted with surprise. She brushed a loose curl from her eyes with the back of her hand and smiled.

In a most subdued manner, she spoke. "Hello."

The man stared at her with piercing brown eyes, as if he were searching for an explanation. He was an imposing figure, six-foot-two inches tall and every inch of him was muscle. He had broad shoulders, dark brown hair, and was ruggedly handsome. His arms were tanned from the sun and his shirt could not hide the bulging muscles rippling across his shoulders and chest.

Melinda guessed that he was about thirty years of age and the sight of him took her breath away. His thumbs were tucked behind his belt as he stood watching her and he had a slight smile on his face, as if he were amused by her actions.

Here she was, a grown woman, wading in a stream of water like some child. She was so embarrassed. Suddenly she felt warmth creep into her face. She began to worry that she might have intruded somehow. Feeling a bit intimidated by his stature and muscular build, she tried to get her courage up. She took a deep breath and then plunged in with her first question.

"Have I trespassed onto private property, sir? If so, I didn't mean to." She waved a hand in the direction she came from and explained, "I climbed the fence back there. I guess I should have known better."

When the man realized he was staring, he looked embarrassed about it and quickly answered in a soft, deep voice. "No, no. It's all right. My cows graze in this pasture and I was going to round them up for milking. I'm sorry if I startled you."

Melinda noticed that his tone was apologetic and could not think of a thing to say.

"Don't worry. Everything's fine. Please stay as long as you like."

For some reason, his face was flushed and he seemed to be flustered as he spoke. Then, without another word, he abruptly turned and briskly strode away.

Feeling confused about why he had acted so flustered, Melinda curiously watched him stride down the field. She could not help but wonder who he was. His voice was soft and kind, his features and mannerisms were rugged, and his eyes were gentle. What a combination! But why did he seem so flustered?

Looking down at her wet feet and legs, she gasped and quickly dropped her skirt. No wonder he had acted so embarrassed. A respectable young woman would never reveal her bare feet, let alone her legs. She laughed softly to herself. How could she have forgotten her upbringing? Was it being out in the open air, feeling free and unfettered from the stifling life of the city? If so, she liked this new feeling of freedom and was happy to be a part of this wild country.

Noticing the sun setting, Melinda realized that she had stayed out a little too long. Quickly, she stepped out of the stream and ran toward her shoes. She sat upon the ground to put them on and once again thought about the quiet stranger she had met. Who was he? Was he an example of what all men out west were like? Were all men this tall and rugged looking? Remembering his frame, she grinned. Were all men in the West that well built? If so, she was going to love the West. Back east, she had never seen such a man before. This was so different from the city! In fact, there seemed to be more than just the scenery that was different about the West.

Remembering his dark eyes and quiet mannerisms, she smiled and thought she might like to get to know this man a little better.

At the dinner table, she asked her aunt and uncle whose property she had just intruded upon. Maybe she could discover something about this rugged-looking stranger without sounding too interested in him. Aunt Martha seemed to know everybody in the community. Her aunt placed her fork on the side of her plate and began.

"His name is Gilbert Roberts. He owns a ranch down yonder and has acres of land. He's a dairyman and a rancher. He has a hired man that milks the cows, but he works alongside him. He's a real good person to his hired help, I hear. If anyone gets in a pickle, he's right there ready to help out." Martha shook her head solemnly and continued. "He's a widower, too, but he doesn't seem to socialize much, I'm told. Has a daughter about eight years of age. His wife died in childbirth. They had only been married for about a year when she died. It was real sad. He's been alone ever since and had to raise his girl without any help. He's real independent when it comes to being a father, I hear. He never asks for help and likes it that way."

She passed the potatoes to Melinda and smiled. "You'll probably have his girl in your class. Some people say that because he has no wife, his girl has gone wild. Personally I think she's a sweet young thing. Her name's Jenny and I hear that she gets in a few fights at school, a real feisty young girl. The last teacher said that she was a real troublemaker."

Melinda listened carefully. She felt sorry for this rugged-looking man, but she did not want to become interested in a person with a problem child, especially one who had been married before. She had had enough of the married men she met at the university; they were all so opinionated and stubborn, not believing in education for women and having little respect for her, and she was fed up with such narrow-mindedness. Men who had been married before seemed to be set in their ways and resented change, not believing in an equal partnership in marriage. Their only expectation was that women should marry and bear children for their husbands. They would often remind her that it was about time she settled down and learned to cook instead of going to college or teaching, and this infuriated her. Melinda's education was important to her, almost as important as equality between the sexes.

She knew that she was making a judgment about Gilbert, but she could not help it. Gilbert had been married before; therefore, he would most certainly be opinionated and stubborn. She would never marry a man who would attempt to "put her in her place," and that was that.

So she quickly dismissed the idea of getting to know this rugged man. But somehow, she felt drawn to him and had no idea why. Maybe it was his quiet demeanor and soft-spoken voice. Maybe it was his embarrassment and boyish attitude as he became flustered and quickly turned and left. Perhaps it was his muscular build that intrigued her. She grinned inwardly. Then she shook her head. No. No matter what, she was not interested and that was that.

Chapter 4
THE TROUBLED CHILD

"The first day of school and what shall I wear?" she thought as she pulled her hair into a soft bun. Melinda felt like a child going to her first day of school, worried that her students would not accept her. She chose a pink muslin dress to wear and quickly ran downstairs and into the kitchen for a bite to eat, and then out the door she ran with her books in hand.

After arriving at school, she placed a notebook and a yellow pencil at each desk. The color yellow was new. Usually the pencils were wooden with no color at all, but the pencil manufacturers had recently decided to color the pencils yellow for a very good reason. The best graphite for pencils came from China. American pencil manufacturers wanted to let people know that their pencils contained Chinese graphite, and in China, the color yellow represented royalty and respect. So, American pencil manufacturers decided to paint their pencils bright yellow, both to advertise their association with China and to represent respect.

Nervous, Melinda stood in front of her desk, quietly awaiting her students. They seemed to trickle in one at a time and then a few more came in bunches, laughing and talking as they found their seats. They sat down and folded their arms, staring at her and waiting to see what she would say. Melinda felt as if she were on trial and waiting to be judged.

The children ranged in age from six to fifteen, and Melinda knew that she would have to divide the children up to teach them. Looking into their faces and yearning to be accepted, she took one step toward the students.

"I'm Miss Gamble. I come from Boston, Massachusetts, and I used to live by the Atlantic Ocean. How many of you have seen the ocean?"

All of them shook their heads in the negative.

"Well, when you look out on the ocean, you see nothing but water as far as the eye can see. It's not like Bear Lake where you can see land on the other side. And when you walk along the beach, you can find shells strewn before your feet, lying on the white sand. If you take a bucket along, you can pick them up and collect them. Usually they are small shells and many are broken from the pounding of the waves."

Melinda held up a conch shell for everyone to see. When she saw the interest in their eyes, she began to relax. Then she walked past each of the students to let them feel the smoothness of the shell. As she walked toward the back of the class, she noticed the edge of a desk behind the book-shelf. Peering around the shelf, she was surprised to see a young student sitting at the desk with her head lying upon her arms. Her eyes were closed.

With a calm voice, Melinda asked, "What are you doing here? Why is your desk separated from the rest of the students?"

One of the students said, rather snobbishly in Melinda's opinion, "That's where she's supposed to sit."

"Why?" Melinda was startled by such an answer.

"Our last teacher told her that she had to sit there from now on and she can't sit with the other students. She's a troublemaker, he says. She has to be out of sight until she can learn to behave."

Another student volunteered, "And she fights with other kids, too."

Another student stood and pointed accusingly at the young girl. "And she doesn't want to learn, either. She just sits there and won't say a thing. She won't open her book and she won't do her lessons. She doesn't write or read. All she does is frown."

Melinda was shocked that a teacher would actually isolate this child from the rest of the class. She was appalled that he would tell the rest of the students that she was a troublemaker and degrade her in front of her peers. How could a teacher do such a thing? What kind of example was he setting about the acceptance of others? She was infuriated by this new knowledge.

"No wonder she frowns. If I were treated like this, I would frown too. Class, I have put notebooks and a pencil on your desk. Will you please write down your feelings about your first day at school? Those who haven't learned to write yet may draw a picture instead."

Melinda knelt down and looked at the young girl. She had opened her eyes and was staring at her desk in defiance. She had on a very pretty blue-flowered dress and her blond hair was neatly braided in the back. Her face was clean and her blue eyes seemed angry.

"What's your name?" Melinda asked in a gentle tone.

The girl said nothing but just glared at Melinda. She knew that this girl had been treated badly by another teacher and now she must try to undo all of that in order to earn this girl's trust. Apparently she was taken care of at home because she was clean and neat. But what was making her so angry? Was it the rejection of the other students or a problem at home?

Once again, she spoke to the young girl. "My name is Miss Gamble. I will be your new teacher from now on. What is your name?"

The girl turned her head toward the wall and did not answer. Rebelliousness was written all over her face. One of the students turned around and said, "Her name is Jenny. She won't talk. She usually doesn't."

Melinda raised her eyebrows. So, this was Jenny. Looking at the other students writing diligently, she wondered what to do. Then, looking at the young girl at her desk, she decided to try another method. Knowing that she needed some private time with her, Melinda dismissed the students for ten minutes of free time outside. The class cheered and ran out to play. After the last student left, Melinda looked into Jenny's eyes.

"Jenny, what is your favorite color?"

Jenny stared at the wall, her mouth pursed tightly in a straight line and her eyes full of defiance.

"Mine is pink and lavender. I like those colors, so I usually pick those colors for my dresses. How about you?"

Still no answer.

"Is it blue? You have on a very pretty dress, Jenny. I love the blue flowers. And you have very pretty blue eyes, the color of the lake here. Your favorite color must be blue. Is that right?"

The hard, angry look in her eyes began to soften. Jenny looked at Melinda and nodded curtly.

At last she got a response. That was a beginning. Melinda stroked the softness of Jenny's hair and said, "Your hair is so pretty. When I was little, I wanted to have hair the color of wheat, just like yours. But look what color it is. I just say it's dark brown, but others argue that it's dark auburn. To have hair the color of wheat is very lucky, Jenny." At last a slight smile came to Jenny's lips. "And, Jenny, it's braided so nicely. Who braids it? Your mother?"

Oh no. Melinda instantly remembered that Aunt Martha had mentioned Jenny did not have a mother. She had stuck her foot in her mouth. Now what? The last thing she wanted to do was make Jenny feel bad.

The corners of Jenny's mouth began to gradually turn upwards. "No, I don't have a mother. Pa does it. I tried once but it looked messy and so I've got to keep trying, Pa says. He says to not give up."

Melinda was elated. She was able to break the barrier between them. "Your father is right, Jenny."

Melinda knew that her next question would be personal, but she needed to know. If things were not right at home, that could be another problem that Jenny would bring to school. She needed to know if Jenny was mistreated or not.

"Is your pa a good father and do you love him?"

Jenny's eyes brightened with love and she smiled at Melinda and nodded. Melinda could tell that Jenny loved her father very much and she sighed with relief.

"I'm glad. Where do you live, Jenny?"

Melinda knew approximately where Jenny lived, but she needed Jenny to talk to her. If she could get her to communicate, then she would be making progress.

In a most quiet tone of voice, Jenny answered, "On a ranch not too far from here on the south side of town."

Melinda lowered her eyes and said quietly, "I'm sorry about your mother. I didn't mean to pry."

Jenny grinned with amusement, as if trying to stifle a giggle. "That's all right. I never knew her."

"So, Jenny, what's your favorite subject in school?"

Instantly the mood changed and the corners of Jenny's mouth turned down into a frown. She blurted out with anger, "Don't have one."

"But there must be something that you like in school."

Jenny's frown remained and the defiance in her eyes was returning as she quickly shook her head.

When Melinda noticed that Jenny's attitude had changed, she decided to change the subject to a more positive one. Apparently school was the wrong subject, so she decided to approach it differently. She wanted Jenny to speak with happier tones in her voice, so she decided to ask her about the people she loved. "Do you have a grandmother or grandfather nearby?"

"My grandpa and grandma live in the East. I don't get to see them often. And my other ones live in Salt Lake City and that's my pa's folks."

"Do they want you to go to school and learn?"

Jenny's eyes looked down at the floor and she had a sober look on her face. "Yes, they do."

"Jenny, how about if we move your desk up here by my desk and you can be my helper? What do you think about that? I really need help at times, like passing out papers or books or to have someone write something on the board for me." Melinda touched Jenny's hand tenderly and asked, "Would you like to be my inkwell monitor? I can help you until you learn the knack of it. I've got a thick old apron for you to wear when you fill the inkwells so you won't get any stain all over your beautiful dress. What do you say?"

Jenny's face beamed with a smile and her cheeks warmed to a rosy color. Then she nodded with a sparkle in her eyes. Melinda could see the pleasure in her eyes as she looked at her. This new assignment would help Jenny feel important and give her more self-confidence. And that, Melinda sensed, was needed at this time.

Quickly, Melinda picked up the desk and moved it toward the front and sat it next to her desk. "How about this spot, Jenny? Is this all right with you?"

Jenny nodded with a beautiful smile on her face. Then Melinda placed a notebook and yellow pencil on her desk and said, "This is just in case you might want to write something. It's up to you, all right?" In giving her the freedom of choice, maybe she would not rebel against learning.

Jenny nodded.

Melinda called the class in and everyone settled down at their desks. One of the students called out, "Why is Jenny sitting there? She's not supposed to. The other teacher placed her at the back and she's supposed to be there so we don't have to see her."

Melinda saw how hurt Jenny's face was at that comment and it infuriated her. She had to stop this sort of treatment immediately. She said in a stern tone, "I'm the teacher. Your other teacher is not here and I have replaced him. I have my own set of rules. He has his. But my rules do not agree with his."

Then a thought came to her and she decided this was a time to teach a valuable lesson. "Class, I'm going to teach you something that I learned at a church meeting one day. I can't remember who said it, but I believe you'll get the gist of it." Melinda walked up to the board and wrote in large bold letters, "I love you even if you spit on me every day. I would love you even more because you need it more.— Anonymous"

She heard a few chuckles and giggles come from the students as she wrote on the board. Turning to look at the class, she asked them, "What does this mean to you?"

One student raised his hand. "It means that if someone is mean to you, that you should still love him."

"You are correct. Everyone needs love. If someone hurts us or spits on us, then maybe he needs more love because he's hurting inside and we don't know it. Maybe he's being rude or mean just to hide his hurt feelings inside. Do you understand?"

Then she pointed to a young man and asked, "What if you were asked to milk the cows and the cow kicked your bucket over and spilled all the milk, and all that hard work was for nothing? Would you be calm about it? I doubt it. Many times when things go wrong with us, we strike out at the first person we see. And many times we strike out at the ones we love. In other words, those who spit on us need more love instead of more anger. I want you to remember this and I want you to learn to love every one of your classmates. Please take out your pencils and notebooks and copy this statement that I have written on the board. Then memorize it."

Melinda walked to her desk and sat down, already feeling discouraged. With her elbows leaning on the desk, she placed her hands over her face so she could relax. Teaching was not as easy as some would say. Could she do some good in the world and make a difference in anyone's life here in the West? The tension was building up inside her and her shoulders began to ache. As she sat quietly thinking with her face resting on her hands, she heard the scribbling of a pencil next to her desk. Looking up, she saw Jenny sitting at her desk and actually writing what she had written on the board. Melinda fought back the tears that welled up in her eyes. Jenny did want to learn.

Melinda decided not to give a lesson that day, and instead had the children tell the class what they liked and disliked, and what their favorite books and hobbies were. She wanted to get to know each of the students well and maybe they would get to know one another better, too. Maybe they would get to know Jenny, just as she wanted them to. Before long, Jenny was standing before the class and telling them what she enjoyed doing most on the ranch.

Jenny said proudly, "I like to go riding on my horse with my pa to round up the cattle."

One of the children gasped, "You have your own horse?"

"Yes, my pa gave her to me. But he makes me brush her down every day and I have to take care of her. He says that when you have an animal, you have to take the responsibility of taking care of him." Jenny sounded enthusiastic as she spoke of her horse and her responsibilities.

Just before Melinda let the students go for the day, she smiled at them and said, "I have learned a lot today. I learned that some of you like to fish, to swim in the lake, to play ball, and even to ride a horse. I also learned that some of you don't like to milk cows, to sweep floors, and do dishes. I learned that some of you have brothers and sisters and some don't. Now would you like to know something about me?"

The students nodded enthusiastically.

"All right, then." Melinda began walking up and down the aisles as she spoke, looking at each student as she passed. "I like doing dishes and cleaning the house but I dislike cooking. My favorite subject in school is music. I love to sing and I'll teach you a song every day. Just before we leave today, I want to teach you a song called 'Clementine.' Do any of you know this song?"

Some shook their heads and others nodded.

Melinda walked to the front of the room and taught the class one verse at a time. As they sang, Jenny listened carefully and watched her teacher but did not participate and sing with the class. After going through the song a couple times, Jenny's confidence rose and she began to sing. In no time at all, Jenny's voice rang out with joy and excitement. She was not on key most of the time, but that did not matter to Melinda. She had broken the barrier between them. With joy swelling in her heart, she listened as the class sang out:

38

Oh my darlin', Oh my darlin',
Oh my darlin' Clementine.
You are gone and lost forever,
Oh my darlin' Clementine.

Chapter 5
BILLY'S PRANKS

The following day, Melinda arrived at school and found Jenny in a fight with Billy. They were squabbling on the ground and the young boy was yelling for help. Melinda eyed Jenny in amazement. Here she was, only eight years old, fighting with a ten-year-old boy. The most shocking part was that Jenny was on top of him, pulling his hair ferociously as he screamed in pain. How in the world, Melinda wondered, did this feisty young lady manage to overpower a boy almost twice her size? Jenny was slender and wiry and Billy was a bit chubby and slow of movement, which could have been a factor. But still, the boy had bulk on his side.

"Jenny!" Melinda called out with her hands on her hips. She was shocked at such behavior. As a new schoolteacher, she felt completely unprepared for what was happening before her very eyes.

No one paid attention. Annoyed, Melinda tried to pull them apart. As she tugged Jenny away, the young man held his face with his hands while Jenny continued to swing her fists at him.

"I'll teach you," yelled Jenny. The blood was rushing through her veins, making her face red with anger.

"Jenny!" Melinda made use of her best tone of authority. "Come with me."

Taking the feisty little she-cat by her hand, she led her inside the school and sat down at her desk. Jenny looked down at the floor with anger flaming from her eyes.

Melinda was frustrated but she knew that kindness and tenderness went further than scolding. She took a deep breath so she could settle down, and with tenderness in her voice, she spoke to Jenny.

"Jenny, what's wrong?"

Jenny would not speak.

Melinda gently held Jenny's hand in hers and with her other hand she tenderly replaced a blond curl that had come loose from the scuffle and was hanging in her eyes. When she saw the defiance in Jenny's eyes, Melinda felt discouraged. Everything she had done yesterday had been completely undone by Jenny's classmates today. Taking a deep breath, she sighed. Then, after uttering a silent prayer, she spoke softly.

"Sweet, sweet Jenny. What am I going to do with you? Why can't you talk to me? You know I care about you. Please tell me why you were fighting with that young man."

Jenny's eyes flamed and she spoke with vehemence in her voice. "He called me a name. He always calls me names every day. I hate him."

"What name did he call you?"

"He called me stupid and dummy and I'm not."

"Of course you're not. You're a very smart young lady with a very pretty smile."

When Melinda smiled, Jenny's frown gradually disappeared and her eyes softened.

"Jenny, you've got to control your temper. Ignore what the kids say because none of it is true. Remember, you are above those who call you names if you just turn and walk away."

Melinda knew that it was easier said than done. After the class settled down, Melinda worried that the children had made their judgments about Jenny simply because of a teacher who announced to the class that she was a troublemaker and had placed her at the back of the class, hidden from the rest of the students. Had he actually said that she was a troublemaker in front of the class? That was what the children had told her. Yet even if he had not mentioned it aloud, then his attitude had demonstrated it. How could she undo every negative word or action the first teacher had inflicted upon her students?

The first two weeks went by quickly. Jenny continued to fight with the boys, but less frequently because she wanted to please her teacher. Each day Melinda would have to give a lecture to the class about respecting one another. Each day she made a conscious effort to build up Jenny's self-esteem. And Melinda knew that Jenny's love for her was growing day by day.

One morning, when all the students were supposed to be reading, one of them made a spit wad and tossed it at Melinda. She knew it was one of the older children trying to be funny and she suspected it was Billy, so she simply ignored it. Then another spit wad was tossed and it hit Melinda's hair and bounced off onto the floor.

With all the patience she could muster, she stood and looked at the class and said sternly, "If I feel another spit wad hit me, then we'll put our books away and we'll get out our math and do a few pages." Then she sat down and all was silent. Another spit wad was not tossed again. The threat of doing extra math was sufficiently frightening.

One day, Melinda noticed that Billy was acting quite mischievous and had tried to dunk Peggy's pigtail in his inkwell. He must have thought his new teacher was dense, she mused. Did most students seem to underestimate their teachers like this? Did he actually believe that she would think it was an accident? When he tried to dunk the braid in the ink, Peggy must have felt him tuck at her hair because she whirled her head around and her pigtail slapped Billy right in the face, swiping his face with blue ink.

Billy had a blue streak across his face for several days and he swore that he would never do such a thing ever again if Miss Gamble would not punish him. Melinda was frustrated and considered a punishment, but opted not to since his blue face seemed to be humiliating enough.

Sometime after the ink incident, Peggy found a frog in her lunch pail. After she screamed at the top of her voice, she headed right for Billy and accused him of placing it there. It seemed to be his style and she was convinced that he was getting even because she whipped his face with her hair. Most everyone suspected Billy to be the culprit because he grinned when she accused him of it—but no punishment was executed since there was no proof of it.

The frustration of being a teacher was high and Melinda wondered if she had made the right decision in coming to the West. Was she doing any good or even making a difference in the lives of any of these children? Their behavior was very discouraging and Melinda found herself weeping at times. But suddenly one day, things began to turn around as if she were being rewarded for her efforts. The third week of school, Jenny began doing her schoolwork and did not act rebellious about it. She had warmed up to Melinda and the joy Melinda felt was incredible. But that was not all!

Melinda had been teaching the history of Bear Lake Valley to her students. "Class, there is a special trail that passes through Bear Lake Valley. It's the Oregon Trail. In 1843, the first wagon train that crossed the Oregon Trail was dubbed the Great Migration. After twenty-five years, more than a half million people went west on this trail. In 1869, there were no more wagon trains because the railroad was completed." She walked up one of the aisles and stood in front of Billy and then continued. "The Shoshone, Ute, and Bannock tribes, plus many mountain men, used the Bear Lake Valley for hunting grounds before the settlers came here. Many Rendezvous were held at the south end of the valley near Bear Lake in the 1820s. Jim Bridger and Jedediah Smith attended those Rendezvous." She eyed the class carefully and asked, "Class, have you ever heard of a Rendezvous before?"

Melinda walked around the room and looked at the children as she spoke. She had a plan that she believed would bring joy and learning to these students and she was about to spring it on them. Taking a deep breath, she continued with her lesson.

"A Rendezvous was a gathering where fur traders, Indians, suppliers, and mountain men met to trade for traps, supplies, furs, guns, and beads. I think it would be very interesting to have a Rendezvous of our own. What do you think? We would bring what we didn't want from home and then we would trade with one another just like the traders did at the Rendezvous. We can even dress up like the mountain men and traders, if you like. Some of you can even dress like the Indians did. Would you like to do that?"

Excitement filled the air as they planned their Rendezvous for the first of November. It would give them time to put together their costumes and find trinkets that they wanted to trade. This would help them get to know one another and learn at the same time. The Rendezvous would take place within the schoolroom since the weather would be too chilly to hold the event outside.

Melinda was so impressed with Jenny. She had come a long way and she was very smart. Melinda wanted the class to get to know Jenny better in an atmosphere other than the classroom, so she decided to plan an excursion that would take the students away from the monotony of the school and hopefully allow them to overcome their prejudices against Jenny.

"Class, I have decided to take you up into the West Mountains to the Paris Springs next Monday. I will show you where the fresh unpolluted water pours out of the mountain and where we get our drinking water from. You will need to bring a note from your parents for permission and a clean cup to scoop up the fresh spring water."

After Melinda told the class about the fun Rendezvous they would have in November and the little excursion in the mountains, Billy seemed to turn pale and became very nervous. Melinda had noticed that his respect for her was gradually growing, but he still seemed to feel the need to torture the girls in class.

Melinda told the class to begin reading and she sat down at her desk. As she sat, Melinda noticed that Billy seemed to be quite fidgety and he kept glancing up at her as if something was on his mind. What was wrong with him? Billy stood and slowly walked up to Melinda with a sheepish look on his face.

He ran his fingers through his brown wavy hair and then he took a deep breath and said, "Miss Gamble, you are making school fun for us and I never had fun at school before. You are much nicer than the other teacher we had. So, I just want to tell you that I'm sorry for all the mischief I've been doing."

"Thank you, Billy. I appreciate that."

"And I'm sorry for what I did today, too."

"Sorry, Billy? You haven't done anything today."

His dark brown eyes widened. "Oh yes I have, Miss Gamble."

She lifted her eyebrows slightly. "What did you do?"

"Well," Billy swallowed and wiped his hands on his pants nervously. "I would like it very much if you would just look the other way while I get something from your desk. All right, Miss Gamble?"

Melinda looked into Billy's eyes questioningly. "Billy, did you put something in my desk?"

"Yes, ma'am."

"Can I peek?"

"No, ma'am. You wouldn't like it if you did. Just turn the other way so you won't get scared, all right?"

Melinda quietly rose from her seat and backed up to the wall so she could watch at a safe distance. Billy opened her drawer and exposed a nice fat garter snake that was lying upon her papers. Billy slid his hands under it and took it out, just as Melinda gasped.

Billy looked up at Melinda and said, "He wouldn't have hurt you, Miss Gamble. He's just a garter snake. I play with them all the time. Pa says that they eat the bad bugs in our garden."

When the girls looked up from their reading and saw what Billy had in his hands, the classroom became a siren of screaming noises that would have pierced the ears of anyone who entered the classroom. It took quite a while to settle the girls down before they could continue with their studies. One girl fainted and another ran outside without permission. The boys laughed until their sides ached, and Melinda wondered if she should give Billy a punishment. Since he had been so honest with her and took the snake outside of his own volition, she hesitated to do so. Honesty had its merits.

Chapter 6
A STUBBORN MAN

One by one, the permission slips arrived on her desk. By the end of the week, Melinda counted them up and found one note was missing. Jenny had not brought her note from home.

While the students worked on their math, she took the opportunity to ask Jenny why she did not bring her note. Jenny's desk still sat next to Melinda's, for Jenny liked it that way and she seemed to study better when she was near her teacher. It seemed that she lacked confidence and being near Melinda helped assure her of her abilities.

"Jenny, I need to talk to you."

Jenny's head rose from her work and she smiled at Melinda.

"Jenny, did you forget to bring a note from home?"

"No."

"But I don't have a note here saying you can go to the mountains."

Jenny lowered her head and looked at her desk. "That's 'cause my pa won't let me go."

"Why, Jenny?"

"He says it's too dangerous."

"But I'll be there and we're going to eat our lunches in the mountains next to the spring. I wouldn't let any harm come to you. The other parents have written notes. They seem to think it's all right."

"But my pa doesn't think so." Jenny looked into Melinda's eyes and frowned. "He never lets me do anything. He says that I might get hurt. The fact is I can't do much of anything, Miss Gamble, because he worries too much. He doesn't want me to wander off alone and he doesn't have time to take me where I want to go because he's too busy."

Jenny looked out the window and spoke as if she were reminiscing about the past. "One time, a neighbor's cat had kittens and she was giving them away and my pa was too busy to take me to her house to get one because he said he didn't have the time." She turned and looked at her teacher with soberness and a bit of sadness in her eyes. "When Pa finally had extra time, all the kittens were given away and it was too late. I wanted a kitten so bad."

"Do you have any little pets at all?" Melinda asked curiously.

Jenny shook her head.

Melinda's heart went out to Jenny and she wanted to help. She knew that the formative years of a child were very important and having a pet was essential to her growth so she could learn responsibility. Melinda also knew it was a part of life and helped with the shaping and development of a child's character. She remembered all too well.

She had learned firsthand how a small animal was able to help a child emotionally. The memory of it warmed her soul as she remembered her childhood days, and how her faithful dog had helped her through many a tough time as she poured her feelings out to him. She remembered how this loving animal had licked her tears away and then snuggled up close as if to comfort her. She remembered the softness of his fur against her face and the enormous amount of love she had for this animal. Her dog had been her friend, her confidant, and had remained faithful to the end. Why hadn't Jenny's father cared enough to go with her to get a kitten?

"Jenny, is it all right with you if I talk to your father and ask his permission for you to go on this trip?"

Jenny looked doubtful that her father would give in, but it was worth a try. "Yes, but it won't do no good."

"You mean that it won't do 'any' good, Jenny."

"Yup. That's what I said."

Melinda smiled and let the English lesson go for now.

The following day was Saturday and Melinda got ready to visit Jenny's father. She wore an attractive lavender muslin dress that fit perfectly on her slender figure. It had puffed sleeves and was gathered at the waist, hanging gracefully over her hips. As she pulled her hair loosely upon her head, she tried to think of what she should say to Jenny's father.

It did not take long to arrive at Mr. Roberts's home. It was a large, beautiful house and the grounds were neat and clean. The house had shrubs around it and there was a small lawn in front. She reined in the horse and, holding her skirts with one hand, stepped down from the carriage.

Melinda looked up and found Gilbert standing on the porch, leaning against the post with his arms folded across his chest, watching her intently. She could tell that he was a very strong man as she glanced at the many tanned muscles in his arms. Trying not to stare at his bulging biceps, Melinda walked gracefully toward him. As she approached, she noticed that he was watching her carefully in a curious manner.

"Mr. Roberts, I'm here about Jenny. I'm Miss Gamble, her teacher."

Gilbert's eyes widened in disbelief and his eyebrows lifted. "You're Jenny's teacher? You're the one I saw at the creek walking barefooted right in the middle of the stream."

Melinda blushed with embarrassment. "Yes, I'm afraid I was and I should have asked permission from you since it was your property."

"No harm done."

Wiping her hands nervously against her skirt, she continued. "Speaking of permission, I'm here to get permission from you to take Jenny to the mountains."

"I'm real glad the way you've been treating my Jenny. You're a real good teacher, better than the other one she had. She likes you and talks about you a lot. But, Miss Gamble, I can't give permission."

"Why not?"

"Too dangerous." His eyes narrowed as he stared at her, as if challenging Melinda to contradict him.

"I would never take the children into harm's way," she insisted. "And the other parents have given permission. They must think it's all right. So, please won't you…"

Gilbert dropped his hands to his side, apparently annoyed with her persistence. "Miss Gamble, I thank you for this visit, but I must go now. I have work to do." Then he stepped down from the porch.

Melinda felt that she could not allow him to leave until she had told him exactly how she felt. She immediately raised her voice a bit and said firmly, "Mr. Roberts, please don't leave. I want Jenny to go. Please listen to what I have to say."

Gilbert was clearly surprised by her persistence but he turned around to face her, folded his arms across his chest once again, and looked at her intently as she spoke.

Looking at his imposing frame, she swallowed. "Mr. Roberts, Jenny needs to feel like she's part of the class. These children have shunned her just because their former teacher was judgmental and helped them to form wrong opinions about her. I want to undo all that. I want her to be accepted. But she needs to socialize with these students in a fun atmosphere outside the classroom. Please let her go."

Gilbert gazed into Melinda's eyes as she spoke and he began to grin. "That was a nice speech, Miss Gamble. But it doesn't lessen the fact that she might get hurt."

"Then come with us to the mountains."

Gilbert raised his eyebrows. "Me? I'm too busy." Then he turned and started toward the barn in large strides.

Melinda became frustrated with his attitude and quickly picked her skirts up and followed him. As soon as she caught up to him, she asked, "Mr. Roberts, is this your answer to everything? When you are done talking, then you simply walk away whether or not the other person is done talking?"

"Are you still here, Miss Gamble?" Gilbert asked, as if wearied by her presence.

"Yes, and I'm not leaving until we talk about this further." Melinda was slightly out of breath as she tried to keep up with Gilbert's fast pace.

"Miss Gamble, I'm done talking."

"But I'm not." Melinda said with a firm and stubborn tone in her voice.

Gilbert suddenly stopped in his tracks and turned to look into her eyes. Her determination was annoying him greatly. "It seems to me, Miss Gamble, that unless I give in to your demands, you won't leave me alone. Is that correct?"

Melinda did not like the way he put that. But, when she thought about it, he was right. The fact was, she wanted to convince Gilbert that Jenny really needed this outing and she was fairly certain that she could convince him of it.

Without waiting for her answer, Gilbert turned and continued striding toward the barn.

"Mr. Roberts, please wait," Melinda begged as she tried to catch up to him. "You said that you won't come with us to the mountains because you are too busy."

"That is correct, Miss Gamble."

"Isn't your daughter more important than work?" It had come out sharper than she had planned but she was not sorry and continued. "It's only a half-day away from work. Isn't your daughter worth it?"

Melinda had emphasized the words "worth it" in a firm tone of voice, hoping he would get the point and respond to it. But the response she had triggered was not what she had expected.

He had gotten the point all right because suddenly Gilbert came to an abrupt stop and stared into Melinda's eyes. His broad chest seemed to puff out and his eyes were cold. He stood rigid and unbending. His jaw became stiff and his voice was stern.

"This is none of your business. My relationship with my daughter is no concern of yours, Miss Gamble." He had snapped at her, and Melinda unconsciously took a step back.

She took a deep breath and regained her courage. Then, with firmness and determination in her voice, she continued, "Oh, but I beg to differ with you, Mr. Roberts. The way you treat your daughter affects her behavior and she brings it to school with her. She brings her joy, her frustrations, her disappointments, and her happiness with her each day. I see it in her eyes when she arrives at school. She is a very happy little girl when she first arrives from home and then the children will pull her down. Suddenly she's not the same person anymore. I'm trying to change all that, but I can't do it alone. I need your help."

Gilbert searched her face as she spoke and did not say a word.

Melinda stared into his eyes, wondering what he was thinking. Had she been too forthright? She had stood up to him and she had not cowered to the firmness of his voice. Was this affecting him in some way? She had pulled her shoulders back and spoke with confidence. Perhaps no one had ever spoken to him in this manner before and he was offended. But that did not matter to Melinda. It was Jenny who mattered.

"Mr. Roberts, please help me," Melinda went on. "I want these children to accept Jenny. Will you accompany your daughter and put your work second just this once? And I promise that I won't ask any more of you." She paused. "Unless it's absolutely necessary."

Gilbert did not take his eyes off Melinda. He breathed in a deep breath and slowly let it out. "You win, Miss Gamble. Besides, it's the only way to get you to leave. I don't need you following me around all day."

Melinda smiled. "Nor would I want to follow you around all day, Mr. Roberts. But if I had to, I would."

"I believe you would, Miss Gamble." Gilbert had a slight smirk on his face, as if he were amused by this unexpected confrontation.

"Thank you very much," Melinda said with a smile. "You will not regret it. Meet us at the school Monday morning at nine thirty." With a big grin, she added, "Wear a jacket and sturdy shoes. It will be a short climb and the mountains will be chilly."

Then Melinda turned on her heels and strode back to the carriage, grinning all the way. She felt like singing. She had won a very important battle.

Gilbert watched her as she walked away from him. "Dad blame it, but she's a stubborn and strong-willed woman," he murmured.

Aside from her strong will, Gilbert had noticed a few things about her that he liked. He liked the way she defended his daughter. Jenny had told him how Miss Gamble would compliment her at school and he liked that, too. Another thing he liked was Melinda's self-confidence and determined attitude. He also noticed how beautiful she was, which was not difficult to see. He noticed her expressive green eyes as she spoke and how they flamed when she was annoyed with him. And last, he noticed how graceful she was as she walked away from him, her skirts swaying with each step she took.

He remembered her delightful laughter at the stream and how happy she had seemed. She seemed unfettered and free, and there had been an almost ethereal beauty about her as Gilbert had watched her walk in the middle of the stream. When she held her skirts above the water, he had noticed her shapely legs and slender ankles as she walked toward him and Gilbert knew he should not have noticed such things, but they seemed to add to her charm.

Chapter 7
THE PARIS SPRINGS

Monday morning arrived and the children were excited about their excursion to the mountains. Jenny's father arrived on horseback precisely at nine thirty. Melinda smiled and walked up to him and said, "You came. I'm glad."

Gilbert grinned. "I had to 'cause I gave my word. I don't back down when I give my word."

"That's admirable," she replied.

Melinda quickly gathered the children together and they hopped into the back of two buckboards that were waiting. Mark was fourteen and had gotten permission to drive his father's buckboard. So, with Melinda in the lead, they headed toward the mountains. It was a dusty five-mile ride, but the children laughed and sang familiar tunes as they headed up the mountain.

Since Paris was situated at the top of the Rocky Mountains, it was not a long drive to the mouth of the canyon. As they rode, they passed one birch tree after another and the pine trees seemed to multiply as they headed up the mountain. The dirt road was rocky and the buckboard bounced and jolted about, but that did not stop the singing and chattering. After arriving at their destination, Melinda grabbed her lunch pail and the children piled out of the buckboard to begin their hike up the mountain.

They only had to walk five hundred yards to the spring, but oh, how lovely this walk was. They passed one quaking aspen after another. There were pine trees, lavender flowers, Queen Anne's lace, and bushes with white berries; shrub after shrub lined their path as they walked. There were scads of yellow daisy-like flowers that were nodding in the breeze on each side of the path, and the white rugged cliffs stood five hundred feet high in front of them, looking magnificent.

While they hiked, Melinda noticed how gentle and attentive Gilbert was with Jenny as he helped her along. She also noticed that he was kind to the other children as well. When they came upon a rugged area, he stopped to help each of the children safely across.

For the first time since Melinda had arrived, Jenny was talking and laughing with the other girls. Melinda had been teaching for one month now and this was the first time she had seen the girls even speak to Jenny. Jenny was laughing and joking as she hiked the hill. Melinda had not heard her laugh before and she thought it was one of the most delightful laughs she had ever heard.

As they walked along the path, Melinda overheard Peggy tell Jenny, "I know that the boys can be rude. But they call all of us girls names, even me. The secret is to ignore them when they do. They just hate it when we don't pay attention to them. I just walk away from them when they start up."

Peggy was a redhead with several freckles on her nose and upper cheeks, and she had a charming smile. She was ten years old and had decided to befriend Jenny. Jenny listened attentively to every word that she said and asked, "They call you names, too?"

Peggy nodded. "Remember when Billy put my braid in the inkwell?"

Jenny giggled and nodded.

"And do you remember the frog in my pail?"

Both girls began to giggle and their laughter bounced off the canyon walls. Melinda knew that this excursion was good for them and she couldn't help but smile at her brilliance.

The swift, white-foamed rapids that rolled over the rocks gradually became louder as they approached the cliff where the water was pouring out of the mountain. As they arrived at their destination, she noticed a large flat boulder in the pathway that led to the springs. Gilbert climbed upon it and then held his hand out to help each child up to the flat boulder. Each girl took his hand to keep balance as Gilbert helped her up, but the boys wanted to be independent and they jumped up to the boulder without any help whatsoever.

Melinda smiled as she saw Gilbert helping the children. He seemed so helpful and caring, and that impressed her. After he helped the last child up, he held his hand out to Melinda. She hesitated as she looked into his eyes.

"Miss Gamble? May I help you up also?"

Gilbert steadily gazed into her eyes with a curious and questioning look. Then Melinda grabbed her skirts with one hand and gave Gilbert her free hand. He held it firmly in his as he helped her up to the flat boulder where he stood. His hand was strong and warm and she blushed from the touch of it, wondering why.

Looking into his eyes, she felt embarrassed and quickly said, "Thank you, Mr. Roberts." Then she walked away toward the children.

Gilbert found it hard not to smile when he saw her face turn a rosy glow as she quickly averted her eyes from his. He seemed to be amused and enjoyed the effect that he had on her. He said, with a slight upturn of his lips, "You're welcome. I'm glad I could help."

Without another thought, Melinda walked to the head of the class and told the children, "Class, follow me."

The roaring sound of the water pouring out of the mountain was exhilarating to listen to, not to mention freezing cold. Melinda encouraged the children to take their cups and scoop the water from the opening where the fresh water was pouring out of the cliff so they could have a drink. This water, she advised them, was unpolluted and fresh from the mountain. They all agreed it was delicious and remarkably refreshing.

As they stood in this small cove between the mountains, a new world opened up around them. It was like a fairyland of greenery that one could only imagine in storybooks and tales. The tall magnificent cliff above them was white with brown and green moss covering the jagged surface. In the river were large moss-covered rocks that were protruding above the water, and dark green shrubs surrounded them on every side.

There was a stream of water pouring out of the mountain and amidst all this was a nest of white butterflies. They flitted about merrily, dozens of them. Gilbert noticed Jenny's immediate interest in God's most beautiful creations, as if a reverent feeling had come over her. She said nothing as she slowly walked toward them and sat down to watch. He continued to watch his daughter's expressions and noticed the effect the butterflies were having on her. How was it that nature could bring such joy to a person?

He watched as Jenny slowly extended a finger out towards them and kept very still. Soon a butterfly landed on her finger and her eyes seemed to smile with delight. He saw her look up at him with a smile, as if hoping he had seen the butterfly on her finger, and he chuckled softly. Gilbert had told her that certain varieties of butterflies would land on a person's finger if one stood still enough, but she had seemed to disbelieve it at the time. And now, she seemed to be testing his knowledge. This made him chuckle even more.

He noticed how still Jenny was sitting and as soon as one butterfly flew off her finger, another one alit. How incredible! This was one of the most peaceful places Gilbert had ever been. No wonder these butterflies had made their home here.

As Melinda looked around, she noticed that it was a sort of wonderland to these children and they were in awe of the beauty that nature had created here. She watched their eager faces and enjoyed seeing their curiosity as they walked around. The children laughed in delight and that made the effort of coming here all the more worthwhile.

This was the first time Melinda had ever spent time in this kind of atmosphere and she could not take her eyes off the magnificence of this view. By looking upon this mountain from the outside, Melinda supposed that none of them had ever guessed that such beauty existed within its walls.

After all of them had dipped a toe or foot into the freezing river and drank their fill of fresh cool water, they took out their lunch and began to eat.

Gilbert sat down beside Melinda and said humbly, "Thank you for asking me to come along. I can see that Jenny needed this little excursion."

Melinda smiled. "You're welcome."

"I'm sorry I was so stubborn at the ranch and gave you such a bad time."

"I understand. Being an only parent can be hard."

He nodded. "I worry about Jenny a lot and I have to make decisions that I think are right."

"I understand. I don't know how you do it—being a single parent. But I do admire your independence in taking care of Jenny. She's an intelligent young girl, but her former teacher made her feel otherwise. I've noticed that she has great qualities. She has a lot of love to share and I believe that you have taught her that."

Gilbert steadily gazed into her eyes as she spoke. He liked what she was saying about Jenny and he enjoyed the pleasant sound of her voice. He noticed how her green eyes seemed to sparkle as she talked. She seemed to be a very positive person and he liked that about her.

"I'll let you finish eating," he said as he rose to his feet. He turned and went back to the rock where he was sitting and watched his daughter as she conversed with Peggy. It was not long until Gilbert was joking around with them and making them giggle.

"If you don't watch out, these butterflies might follow you home like a lost puppy and then what would you do? What would you feed them?"

This made the girls giggle with delight as they tried to search for an answer, but they knew he was teasing them and that made it even more fun. When Melinda saw that the children were done eating, she rounded them up to leave.

Gilbert stood on the ground below the large flat boulder and helped the children down by lifting each of them from the boulder down to the ground where he stood. The older boys did not want help, though. They jumped down from the boulder with excitement and laughter.

After the last child was down, he looked up into Melinda's eyes and asked, "May I help you?"

Melinda nodded and held her hand out for help. But instead, he took her by the waist and lifted her into the air with ease, without exertion, as if she did not weigh any more than the children did. His biceps pressed against the sleeves of his shirt as he lifted her to the ground.

Melinda did not expect this and she gasped as he lifted her from the boulder.

After he placed her on the ground, he said with a twinkle in his eyes, "I wouldn't have dropped you."

Melinda had no comment to make as she tried to get her breath back. Her heart beat rapidly and her face flushed a rosy color. Trying not to let him see her reaction, she quickly turned and strode down the mountain at a fast pace. She did not understand why she was responding this way to the touch of this rugged rancher. Why had he taken her breath away in more ways than one? She didn't even know him.

After getting the children situated in the back of the buckboards, Melinda thanked Gilbert for coming. She whipped the reins and down the mountain they went.

Gilbert stood beside his horse and watched her leave. He had definitely noticed the effect he'd had on her, and it made him grin. It had been a long time since he had made a woman blush. Perhaps he still had what it took after all these years!

He shook his head and puffed out a breath of air and muttered, "Darn that woman. She can get under a man's skin."

Then he climbed onto his horse and headed for home.

Chapter 8
A SELF-WILLED WOMAN

The following day, the students were all abuzz with the adventure they'd had at the mountains. Melinda wrote a thank-you note to Gilbert for helping with the children. Then she passed it around to let the class sign it.

After class was over, she freshened up and borrowed the carriage so she could take the note to Gilbert. Melinda could have given it to Jenny, but for some reason she preferred to take it herself. Perhaps, she thought, it was because she had been so stubborn about having Jenny come on the excursion and she wanted to personally thank him for letting her go. Or, of course, it could have been that she was simply attracted to him. The idea of being attracted to this rugged rancher was nonsense, however. He simply was not her type. If, by some strange turn of events, they *were* to marry, Melinda was certain he would immediately decide to "put her in her place." Since he had been married before, he would be used to a woman waiting on him and would probably make her give up her career in order to better serve him. No, she would marry someone who was independent and would allow her to continue teaching. Quickly she shook the notion out of her mind.

Melinda knocked on Gilbert's door and Jenny answered with a broom in her hand. She was surprised to see her teacher and her eyes lit up.

"Hello, Jenny. May I see your father? I wanted to give him this thank-you note from the class."

Jenny smiled. "Pa's down yonder fixin' the fence. The cattle started gettin' loose yesterday and he found the place they got loose and is fixin' it." Jenny pointed in the direction for her to go.

Melinda thanked her and then turned to leave. As she walked down the pasture, she came upon the stream that she had waded in before school had started. She recognized it immediately because of its unmatched beauty.

Gilbert had one of the choicest pieces of land for cattle to graze and it was a beautiful sight with groves of trees and a stream flowing gently through his pasture. Gilbert had worked hard and had saved enough money to buy this property and the cattle. It took hard work and a lot of time to make this ranch what it was. Gilbert had bought it six years earlier and had put up every inch of fence around it for his cattle to graze.

When the house had been sufficiently cleaned, Gilbert had allowed Jenny to join him on the ranch. He had taught his daughter to ride a horse and shoot a rifle. Gilbert and Jenny were very close and had a bond that most fathers did not have with their daughters. The only thing he was guilty of was being overprotective of her. But, he was an only parent and he did the best he could.

As Melinda stopped to admire the view, she heard a deep warm voice ask, "Are you lost or are you looking for me?"

Melinda quickly turned around and saw Gilbert standing next to a maple tree, looking at her with his thumbs tucked behind his belt. When their eyes met, Melinda felt nervous and tried to search for the right words to say.

"Did you need to talk?" he asked.

"Uhm…no." Melinda took a deep breath and continued. "I just came to give you this." She showed him the note in her hand. "It's from the class. It's a thank-you note for helping us yesterday."

Gilbert took the note from her hand and looked at it. Then he folded it and put it in his pocket.

"You could've given it to Jenny to deliver to me," Gilbert said soberly as he gazed into her green eyes.

"But I wanted to thank you personally."

"Personally, eh?" A restrained smile flickered across Gilbert's face.

Melinda blushed and averted her eyes. She looked at the ground, a little flustered because she felt so clumsy. "Well, you took time off work just to come with Jenny so she could go on the outing with the class and that meant a lot to me…" She hesitated. "That is, it meant a lot to Jenny. I had never heard her laugh until yesterday and it was like music to my ears. Thank you for putting Jenny before your work this time."

Gilbert became sober once again. "I always put my Jenny first. All I do here on this ranch is for her and for her comfort." As he spoke, his tone was a little defensive and she noticed it.

Feeling embarrassed, she tried to apologize for her insinuation. "I'm sorry. I didn't mean that you neglect her, sir. I just meant that sometimes you put your work before Jenny. That's all. And at her young age, her needs are very important. Work should always come second to a child."

"How can you judge me?" Gilbert said with exasperation. "You don't know the sacrifice I make just for my daughter."

Gilbert had an edge in his voice and sounded a little irritated, which flustered Melinda even more.

"I'm sure you sacrifice, but many times we can forget the little things that really matter to a young girl."

"For example?" Gilbert said curtly.

Melinda began to feel nervous. This was not going well at all. She had stuck her foot in her mouth and she did not know how to get it out. How could she avoid the answer to this question? She had no idea, so she decided to just say what was on her mind.

"Such as having a pet."

Gilbert frowned and crossed his arms over his chest. With an indignant tone, he said, "So, you're referring to the kitten she wanted, aren't you?"

"Yes, I am," she said firmly.

Melinda did not like his tone of voice at all. She probably should not have mentioned the kitten, but he had asked and she did not know how to answer without offending him. She was getting into this discussion further than she wanted and could not seem to get out.

Gilbert's jaw became firm as he raised his voice. "The day Jenny wanted to go look at the kittens, a cow was having a calf. I couldn't leave. The cow was having complications and I needed to be here to help. I would have lost both of them if I'd left." Looking down at his feet and back up at Melinda, he snapped, "And why is any of this your concern, anyway?"

Melinda felt embarrassed. She had prejudged him without even thinking. She lowered her eyes to the ground and replied in a soft tone. "I'm sorry, Mr. Roberts. My tongue is too quick. I shouldn't have said anything. It wasn't my place...or my business." She looked up into his eyes with dismay. "But why are you so ornery with me? Why didn't you just explain? You know I really love Jenny. That's why I tell you how I feel and that's why I'm concerned about her."

Frustrated, Gilbert shook his head. "You wouldn't understand."

"Give me a chance."

Gilbert took a deep breath. "I do my best for Jenny. I take care of her and I love her. I don't neglect her for work. I take her along with me wherever I go. She rides her own horse alongside me. But when I decided to take work off yesterday to go to the mountains because you insisted, I came home to find half my cattle loose. It took the rest of the day and most of the evening to round them up. If I'd been here, I could have stopped them before too many escaped. As it was, I had to hunt all over for the weak spot in the fence after rounding up my cattle."

71

As Melinda listened, her heart sank and she felt terrible. She should have been more understanding. She had drawn a conclusion without any facts.

"I...I didn't know. I'm sorry, Mr. Roberts. Please forgive me for being so bold. But you seem to think it's my fault."

Gilbert's frustration began to leave and his eyes seemed to soften when he heard the humility in her voice. Shaking his head, he answered softly, "No, I don't. I don't blame you. I just took it out on you and I didn't mean to. You seemed to be the perfect scapegoat for my frustrations."

Melinda grinned. "It seems every time we meet, we argue about something."

Gilbert laughed in a low pleasant tone. "You're quite refreshing."

"I take that as a compliment."

"It was given as one, Miss Gamble. As I think about it, I've never met a woman who's so darned stubborn and self-willed as you are."

Melinda frowned. "Self-willed?"

Gilbert grinned and nodded. "Yes. If you hadn't persisted, I wouldn't have gone to the mountains. And I did have a good time, too."

With firmness in her voice, she defended herself. "I'm not self-willed. Determined, maybe, but not self-willed. You've misjudged me altogether. There's a difference between determination and being headstrong. You are so rude at times. Mr. Roberts, how can you say that I'm self-willed when you don't even know me?"

Gilbert chuckled. He seemed to find her attitude quite humorous. It did not take much to set her anger aflame.

When she saw him grin, the blood rushed to her face and she was not in the mood for any more talk. "Mr. Roberts, thank you and good-bye. I have more productive things to do today than to stand around here and be insulted by you."

Melinda picked up her skirts and quickly walked toward the carriage with her chin in the air. Self-willed! How she hated that word! Her mother would call Melinda self-willed when she had an idea in her mind and would not give up. Melinda knew that she was self-willed, but she hated it when others reminded her of the fact. She knew her faults and weaknesses and she did not need to be reminded of them.

As she walked toward her carriage, Gilbert watched with interest. What an intriguing woman! She had such grace, even when she was angry, and for some reason that attracted him to her. She was not afraid to speak her mind at all. He burst out into laughter.

"Well, I now know never to tell her that she's self-willed ever again."

Chapter 9
THE GRIZZLY BEAR

The week passed into October and Melinda wondered if she had done any good or made a difference in the lives of anyone yet. As she sat on the bank of the creek at the edge of the West Mountains, she noticed the leaves had turned orange, yellow, and red from the cool nights, and the beauty of it was breathtaking. It appeared as if paints had been spilled upon a canvas and there were blotches of color everywhere. What beauty there was in these mountains!

As she stared at the colorful leaves covering the mountainside, Melinda felt at peace. The river shimmered as the sun danced upon the water. The days were already chilly and she wore a light wrap around her shoulders. Melinda found herself taking a walk almost every day. She found comfort being among nature, where she could think without interruption.

Wispy clouds were floating in the breeze as Melinda walked. Her spirits rose as she journeyed along the hillside.

She strolled to a grove of quaking aspen near the river and sat on a log. The bubbling brook was a soothing sound that filled her solitude with pleasant, fanciful thoughts.

As Melinda sat quietly thinking, something disturbed her reverie. The few birds that were twittering stopped suddenly and flew away. She looked toward a marshy area and saw something moving. She stood and began to slowly walk toward it. To her amazement, she saw a grizzly bear digging and eating roots in the marshy ground near the river. She smiled and was amused at how wild the West really was. But she was not acquainted with the nature of these animals and she was very curious. Melinda stood quietly watching the bear as it was digging for roots. She was about two hundred yards away—a safe distance, she thought to herself.

As she watched contentedly, Melinda heard an irritated grunt as the grizzly raised its head and saw her standing off in the distance. The grizzly snarled with anger as if warning her to leave. Then, almost immediately, it let out a hideous growl and leapt clumsily toward her. Its enormous jaws were spread wide and its eyes were flashing fire. Melinda had never seen anything so frightening in her life.

Fear overtook her and Melinda could not retain adequate presence of mind. Her chest tightened and her face drained as she tried to catch her breath. She panicked and quickly turned and ran as fast as she could go. Her heart was pounding rapidly with each step she took. She felt as if she were running in slow motion. Surely this was a dream. No, it was more like a nightmare. Suddenly, to her horror, she lost her balance as she tripped over a rock and fell face down on the ground in a cushion of soft weeds and mud.

In the distance, she heard a deafening shot and immediately the bear growled as if in pain. Someone had shot the bear in the right shoulder. Terror filled her soul as she scrambled to her feet. She noticed the bear had lunged to the right, heading toward the man with the rifle. When Melinda turned, she saw Gilbert standing with a rifle in his hand, aiming at the grizzly.

As the bear bounded toward Gilbert, he quickly reloaded his Remington 45-70. Gilbert's heart beat rapidly as he watched the bear run clumsily toward him. When it came within twelve feet of Gilbert, it suddenly stopped and raised its massive body erect, its mouth wide open, showing its enormous teeth. The grizzly gazed at him with fire in its eyes and it gave a blood-curdling roar. With its mouth agape, the grizzly was a savage-looking beast.

Melinda began to scream. She had never seen such a hideous sight before and she became paralyzed with fear. The feeling of terror that rose in her throat made it hard to breathe and she began to shake uncontrollably.

The grizzly began walking on its hind legs toward Gilbert. It was an enormous animal, between eight to nine feet tall. Gilbert carefully aimed his rifle at the grizzly's heart and waited. He hated to kill this remarkable animal but he had no choice. The grizzly came within six feet of Gilbert before he pulled the trigger. As the bullet pierced its heart, the bear gave a deathly roar and fell dead at Gilbert's feet.

As Melinda stood shivering, she began to cry uncontrollably from the fear that had built up inside her.

Immediately Gilbert ran toward her, dropped his rifle, and held her in his arms as she wept. He tried to soothe her, but it was to no avail. As she wept, he rubbed her back and shoulders, trying to calm her down and relieve her tension. Then he took his handkerchief out of his pocket and wiped the mud from her face.

With tenderness, he asked, "Shall I take you home?"

Melinda could not answer. She could not even speak. Gilbert knew she was in shock. When he tried to encourage her to leave with him, she did not respond. He looked into her beautiful green eyes and his heart went out to her as he saw the fear that was still in them. So, he swung his rifle over his shoulder and picked her up in his arms and carried her toward his home. Melinda laid her head on his shoulder and stared off into the distance.

When he felt her head resting against his shoulder, warmth filled his heart and he realized that he had not felt the softness of a woman for eight years. He had not courted or even been interested in any woman because he had devoted all his time to Jenny and his ranch.

When he arrived home, he sent Jenny to get a doctor. Then he laid Melinda down on the sofa, got a wet rag from the kitchen, and wiped the rest of the mud from her face. Then he began to gently rub her arms and shoulders, hoping it would relieve her anxiety, but she did not respond to his touch. Gilbert became worried as he observed the blank look on her face.

He noticed that she was still shivering, so he put a blanket over her and tucked it around her body. Then he got a pillow and gently placed it under her head. Gilbert would not leave her side. He was so worried that he pulled up a chair and watched her intently. The concern he felt deepened the lines between his eyes.

"May I get you some water?" he asked.

Melinda did not respond, so he decided to talk to her and tell her any kind of news that came to his mind. Maybe if she thought of something else, she would not think of the attack. Gilbert rubbed her soft hands between his to warm them up as he spoke.

"Did you know they caught Meeks for the bank robbery? They didn't catch Cassidy or Lay, though. I understand that you had to give a description of the bank robbers to Sheriff Davis and give an account of what happened."

Melinda looked up into his face but did not say a word. She shivered for half an hour, but she listened gratefully to the soft deep tones of his voice. After a while, she began to calm down.

"Do you want a drink now?" Gilbert asked.

Melinda nodded and Gilbert quickly got up and brought her a glass of cool water. Then he sat down and watched her drink.

After drinking the water, she looked at Gilbert and with a shaky voice said, "I've never seen such a sight in my whole life. It was the most hideous thing I've ever seen. What did I do to make him so mad?"

Gilbert rubbed his chin thoughtfully. "Well, it could be a variety of reasons. First, you might have startled him, which probably was the reason. If one comes upon a bear, you just quietly walk away. But there are a number of other reasons, too. Such as coming too close to a mother bear's home when she has little cubs. She feels the need to protect her home and family, but I doubt that was the reason."

"Why?"

"For two reasons. Grizzlies usually make their home in the mountains and not in the valleys where people are. I doubt she would have any cubs down this far among civilization." Then he grinned from ear to ear with a mischievous look in his eyes. "And this bear couldn't possibly have cubs since it was a male," Gilbert said in a teasing tone, hoping she would get his little joke.

Melinda got the joke all right and she groaned good-naturedly. "You think you're funny, don't you?"

"Sure do. I need to make this situation light so you'll recover. Talking about recovering, I sent Jenny for the doctor. He should be here anytime."

"I don't need a doctor. I'm not ill."

"Not sick, but mentally stressed and maybe he can give you something to relax you. That wasn't some trivial experience that happened out there. It was a frightful experience for you. It might take a few days to get back to normal."

"Mr. Roberts…"

"Please call me Gilbert."

"Was it your first time shooting a bear?"

"No." He scratched his head, remembering. "One time a bear moved into our area and killed a few sheep and a few calves. A bunch of us had to go after it. Once they begin to kill our animals and get the taste of blood in their mouths, they don't usually stop. So, a few of us had to go out and find the culprit. It's such a shame to kill such a magnificent beast, though. But our cattle and sheep are what we live on and if we let the grizzly get away with it, it won't stop killing."

Gilbert knew one thing, though: bears could not be killed very easily. Many times the bullets did not penetrate deep enough to kill it because of its thick hide. So, he had learned to take careful aim and make sure the shot counted because if it didn't, there was a good chance he would be mauled or killed. He knew the only places to kill a grizzly, for sure, were in the head or in the heart. Anywhere else, and it would not drop immediately.

Melinda was watching Gilbert with curiosity. His eyes were staring off in the distance and he seemed to be deep in thought.

"Mr. Roberts?"

Gilbert's eyes turned toward her. "Yes?"

"I appreciate your help. If you hadn't been out hunting I don't know what would have happened to me."

"I wasn't hunting."

"Why were you in the area with your rifle?"

"Don't know."

"You don't know?"

"Yup. Don't know."

"What do you mean you don't know?"

Gilbert leaned forward, facing her, and rested his arms against his legs. "Well, I live by instinct, so to speak. I felt an urgent feeling come over me and didn't know why. I've noticed that when I don't listen to those feelings, then I'm sorry afterwards. So when I felt this urgent feeling come over me, I just grabbed my rifle and headed out the door. I first walked down to the pasture to see if my cattle were all right and they were, so I just continued northward toward the West Mountains for a ways. It's not too far from my pasture, so when I heard the hideous growling in the distance I quickly ran and made it there just as it began to leap towards you."

"Oh, a premonition."

"Don't know if that's what it is. I just go by instinct mostly."

Melinda steadily watched Gilbert as he spoke. There was something about this rancher that intrigued her and she didn't know what it was. He seemed so rugged, yet there seemed to be something gentle about him at the same time. But one thing she did know was that he was not her type. She was not about to learn how to cook special delicacies for any man. She dismissed the idea of getting to know him altogether. Melinda was his daughter's teacher and that was that. Anything else would not be proper.

Chapter 10
THE DOCTOR

Gilbert's home was a cozy place with the living room, kitchen and dining room all in one room with no dividing walls. The walls were made of dark wood, but no pictures hung there. A sofa and two soft, stuffed chairs faced a rock fireplace on the right side of the room. The kitchen was at the left side of the room with a cabinet that separated the living room and the kitchen. If a person was preparing food, then he or she could communicate with someone on the sofa. The table was near the kitchen end, towards the hall that led to three bedrooms.

While waiting for the doctor, Melinda's mind was in a whirl. After the bear attack, Melinda relived that moment of terror over and over again in her memory. The vision of the grizzly kept haunting her. She felt anxiety rise within her as she thought of it.

Melinda shivered as she realized how close Gilbert had come to being attacked. If he had not aimed carefully enough… She shook her head and quickly put the notion out of her mind. It was too terrifying to even imagine.

The doctor arrived with Jenny and he checked Melinda's heart and the strength of her pulse. Then he mixed some powder in a glass of water and handed it to her to drink.

After a while, he said, "Melinda, you are one lucky lady. If Gilbert had not come along when he did, you would have been mauled so badly that if you'd lived through it, you would have had many broken bones and lacerations. You city folks don't understand the dangers out here in the West. But with time, I guess you'll learn."

Melinda winced at the doctor's words. Then the doctor spoke softly to Gilbert in the kitchen, handed him a bottle of powder, and bid everyone farewell. Melinda pushed the covers off her legs and began to stand up, but her weak knees gave way and she slumped to the floor.

Immediately, Gilbert was at her side. He slid his hands around her waist and lifted her to the sofa. Melinda was aware of his tender touch as he tried to make her comfortable. When she looked into his soft dark eyes, she noticed how concerned he was and it touched her heart.

Then Gilbert said in a worried voice, "You can't get up quite yet. The doctor told me that the medicine he gave you was to relax you and take your anxieties away. He said that you'd get drowsy and I think he's right." He tucked the lightweight blanket around her shoulders. "You'd better rest for a while longer and then I'll take you home on the buckboard."

Then he handed her the powder the doctor had given him and said, "Take this in the evening just before bed. It'll make you drowsy and help you sleep. You've been trauma-tized and he thinks you'll need this at night."

Melinda nodded as she sank into the couch. Her head was cradled in the soft pillow and she closed her eyes. It was not long until she fell into a deep sleep.

While Melinda was sleeping, Gilbert went about his chores. He and Jenny fixed a meal, swept the floor, and set the table.

"Jenny, put on a tablecloth this time." He smiled cheer-fully. "We have a visitor. And our best plates, too."

Jenny smiled back. "I really like my teacher, Pa. She really seems to care about me. The other teacher never did. She makes me feel important."

"I'm glad, Jenny."

Gilbert watched his daughter as she set the table. What his daughter said impressed him greatly. Her teacher cared and she showed it in her actions and words. He walked over to the chair next to the sofa and sat down, watching Melinda sleep. What was it about this Eastern lady that fas-cinated him so? Was it her grit and determination? Was it her kindness to his daughter, whom he adored? Was it her caring attitude towards others? He did have to admit, though, that she was a strikingly beautiful woman and that certainly added to her charm. He wondered why they ar-gued each time they met. Then he thought about their dif-ferences and he shook his head in dismay. An Eastern lady and a rancher were not a good combination, he thought.

Yet he knew that he was attracted to her. It had been years since he had spent time with a woman, let alone held one in his arms. And for the first time in eight years he felt the desire to care for someone other than his daughter. For some reason he felt a need to protect Melinda and he could not deny it. But they were too different and the West was too wild for her. She would probably go back to the East after the school season was over, especially after the grizzly experience. He would be surprised if she even renewed her contract at all.

As her eyelashes began to flutter, he realized she was about to wake up. Gilbert smiled as she opened her eyes and looked up at him. When their eyes met, he asked softly, "Hungry?"

Melinda yawned and stretched every muscle that she had, just to make sure everything was working. Then she nodded.

"Jenny and I made something for you to eat before I take you back home."

Melinda looked over at the table and saw how neatly it had been set. She was going to ask if he could take her home instead, but she realized they had gone to a lot of trouble. And besides, she had never met a man who could cook before. Maybe it would be worth it just to try his food.

She smiled appreciatively. "Thanks. I appreciate it."

As they sat at the table and ate, Melinda noticed what good manners Jenny had. Gilbert had taught her a lot, and he had not forgotten the importance of manners. Each time Jenny wanted to talk about the grizzly and what it looked like, Gilbert would ward off the subject with his eyes and each time Jenny got the hint and let it lay.

After they ate, Gilbert took Melinda home in his buckboard. As they rode in silence, he was conscious of her sitting beside him and he had a feeling of great peace. Once at her house, he reined in the horse and stepped down from the buckboard. He looked up at Melinda and held his hand out toward her. Taking her hand in his, he felt the softness of it and he smiled at her as a warm feeling seemed to engulf him. This woman, of all the women in the world, was managing to have an effect on him. But he and Melinda were just too different and he was certain it would not work out. Why did he have to be so attracted to her?

Melinda stepped down from the buckboard and thanked him for the fine supper. "You're the first man I've ever met who knows how to cook. And thank you for saving my life like a knight in shining armor, sir."

This made him laugh jovially. His laugh was deep and warm and it made Melinda smile. When she noticed Gilbert gazing into her eyes, she felt a warmth creep into her cheeks. What was he thinking?

He took her by the arm and led her to the front door, tipped his hat with his fingers and said, "Miss Gamble, I hope you have a good evening."

As she watched him walk toward the buckboard, she wondered about Gilbert. He seemed to be so rugged on the outside, yet his eyes were gentle and caring. Besides that, this tough man could cook. And he was good at it, too. He was such a contradiction.

Melinda quietly closed the door, intrigued by this mysterious rancher.

Chapter 11
THE DANCE

Uncle William sat in a chair in the living room, comfortably reading the newspaper, while Melinda was upstairs in her bedroom getting ready for the dance. She could hear her aunt and uncle speaking downstairs.

"Martha, listen to this," said William, and began to read aloud from the paper. "Susan B. Anthony has really been working hard for women's rights. A resolution was passed in Idaho. It says, 'Believing in equal rights for all and special privileges to none, we favor the adoption of the pending women's suffrage amendment to the Constitution.' Idaho is now considering giving women the right to vote. Well, I'd say it's about time, don't you think? Why, it was in January of this year that Utah entered the Union as a state, and they introduced women's suffrage immediately. Right now women have full suffrage in only three states and all of them are in the West: Wyoming, Colorado, and Utah. I don't know if it'll go through in time for the November election, though, since it's already October. I'm guessing that it won't."

Martha stood in the doorway of the kitchen, listening. "William, who do you think will win the election this year?"

"Our nation is in such turmoil, Martha," he said, ruffling the pages of the newspaper. "Mills and factories have shut down, merchants are bankrupt, and millions are out of work and have no means of livelihood. Poverty seems to dominate this country. Martha, due to the severe depression we've had, which started during the Democratic administration, I believe that the Republicans will win by a long shot."

Martha picked up a clipping from the kitchen table and walked into the living room. "William, I just read an article in the September *Women's Exponent* by Emmeline B. Wells, the editor and publisher. I clipped it out to keep because it was so inspiring. I'll read it to you. She wrote, 'In this crisis of the present time, women as a class all over the land are manifesting greater interest than ever before, and giving more intelligent thought to public questions and needs. The women of Utah, who have just been given equal suffrage, have a hard question before them to solve, and they should above all else study carefully and prayerfully over these matters that are so new to them, and of such grave importance. Be sure to register properly, and be ready to vote.'" Martha looked over at William and said with a longing in her voice, "I can't wait for Idaho to pass its amendment, William."

Then she called to Melinda, "Are you ready, dear? The town social starts in fifteen minutes. Let's not be too late."

Melinda knew that her Aunt Martha felt that it was time to introduce her to the residents of Paris at the town social that night. Melinda was excited about meeting the townsfolk. She had met a few of the parents of her students during the past two months, and she felt this would be a great opportunity to meet the rest of the people.

As they entered the room, the music and dancing had already started. Aunt Martha began to introduce Melinda to each person she came across. After a while, Martha spied Henry, a handsome young bachelor. "Henry, come here. I'd like to introduce you to my niece."

Henry was a thin and tall young man, about twenty-five years of age, with blond hair and blue eyes. He walked toward Martha and Melinda with a broad smile on his face.

"Yes, Martha?"

"This is my niece and the new schoolteacher in town. Melinda, this is Henry. He's the superintendent of schools. Henry examines prospective teachers' credentials and hires them for the district, in addition to being the janitor and 'fix-it man.' In other words, he was the one who accepted you to fill this position. He will coordinate school activities if needed, and if you need anything at all, you can just ask Henry and he'll get it for you or fix it."

"It's nice to meet you, Henry," Melinda said. "I'm sure I'll be obliged to use your services every now and then."

Henry held his hand out for a handshake and smiled charmingly. "Melinda, I'm glad to meet you at last. I've heard so much good said about you. I'm sorry that I haven't taken the time to come over to the school. I tend to spend an awful lot of time over in Montpelier, helping the teachers with a few problems there."

The three of them were interrupted by the sound of loud and excited voices. They turned and saw a huddle of men surrounding Uncle William, who was showing them a picture of a quadricycle from a magazine. Melinda and Henry moved toward them to see the picture.

William exclaimed with excitement, "The article under this picture says: 'On June 4, 1896, Henry Ford put the finishing touches on his magnificent creation. It is gasoline-powered and Ford calls it the Quadricycle since it runs on four bicycle tires. It took him two years to make it. The Quadricycle is built on a steel frame, and the seat is shaped like a box covered with green cloth and it has metal arms on each side of the seat. The dashboard is made of wood. There is an electric bell in front of the dash and a bicycle lamp is mounted on the side for driving at night.' So, you see, boys, this is going to take the place of horses, I bet."

"Not a chance." One of the men spoke up in a loud voice, emphasizing his disapproval. "I wouldn't ride in one of those contraptions if someone paid me."

"You'll see. This Henry Ford is serious about making more of these quadricycles. And when he starts selling them, I'm going to be the first to buy one."

William smiled as the men guffawed at his silly notion, slapping him on the back with amusement.

Melinda was beginning to think the town social was a wonderful place to meet people. Henry took Melinda in his arms, glided her around the room, and danced several dances with her. He was a good dancer and a very good conversationalist. He seemed to be genuinely interested in her and asked several questions about her and her background. She noticed they had quite a few things in common, too. She surmised that he would make a wonderful friend.

As Melinda socialized, she scanned the room for Gilbert, but he was nowhere in sight. After she thought about it, however, she guessed it was for the best that he was not there. They had nothing in common and it was simply unwise to get involved with a student's parent anyway.

Chapter 12
THANKSGIVING DAY

October gave way to the crisp chill of November, and the schoolchildren had brought things to trade at the Rendezvous. Some had dressed up in buckskin clothing while others wore their school clothes with an Indian blanket wrapped around their shoulders and a brown cloth band tied around their heads. Each child had brought a few things to trade and had his or her own little area set up as a base. The desks were placed on the edges of the room and the center was cleared for walking and trading. Just before they began, Melinda stood in the middle of the room and taught them about the mountain men and the Indians and how they traded with one another. Then she continued her lesson on Bear Lake history.

"Class, I want to teach you one more thing about this area before we begin trading. Pathfinders such as John Fremont and Captain Bonneville wrote of their findings here. Fremont named the mountain peaks, canyons, and streams in the area. And Bonneville wrote of the huge marsh located north of Bear Lake."

Melinda folded her arms as she walked about the classroom and explained, "The Indians lived here first. It was their land and their home. To some, the white man was a guest in their land and they accepted him, but to others the white man was considered a threat. The Indians didn't want them to move into their land and take over. So, in 1863, when the Mormon settlers wanted to settle in this area, Charles C. Rich, under the direction of Brigham Young, went to the Indians himself and asked permission to live here. Why do you think they got permission to live here instead of just moving in?"

Jenny quickly raised her hand and Melinda called on her. "That's simple, Miss Gamble. You see, they didn't want to make trouble with the Indians. It was their land and they needed permission to come here. If they wouldn't have gotten permission, then they might have had bunches of trouble."

Melinda smiled at Jenny's explanation. "That's right, Jenny. They didn't want another war on their hands and there had been several skirmishes throughout Iowa, Nebraska, Wyoming and Utah. When Charles Rich approached the Indians, they had a choice to accept or reject the settlers. After much discussion, the Indians gave permission for the settlers to come here on one condition. They would have to share what they grew and what they had, like cattle and sheep and some of the produce they raised. Charles Rich agreed to it because he believed it was better to feed the Indians than to war with them. In 1864, the settlers moved here and Paris was the first community that was established in the Bear Lake valley. The settlers knew of the agreement that Charles Rich made with the Indians and they agreed to it before coming here."

The trading began and the children were delighted as they traded their wares with one another. It was a day Melinda would never forget as she watched their excited faces and heard them chatter.

A couple of weeks passed and Melinda was excited to spend Thanksgiving Day with her aunt and uncle. The weather was crisp and cold and a fire was made in the fireplace each day. As it crackled and popped, Melinda thought what a pleasant sound it made. It was sort of a homey sound and she liked it. As they busily prepared the turkey, cranberries, and potatoes, Melinda and Martha listened to the soothing voice of Uncle William.

Uncle William was sitting comfortably in a kitchen chair reading to Martha and Melinda from the *Woman's Journal*, a newspaper about women's suffrage published out of Boston, which Melinda had received from her parents that week. Her parents wanted her to keep up with what was happening in the world.

Uncle William seemed to enjoy reading about the events around the world. "Melinda, listen to this," he said with enthusiasm. "Your Boston newspaper has something about Idaho. Listen: 'Welcome, Idaho! State number four has wheeled into line! An unexampled victory for woman suffrage has been achieved in the State of Idaho.' Martha, that means that you can vote next year; and you, too, Melinda, if you renew your teaching contract. You'll be an Idaho State citizen."

Melinda smiled. "Sounds good to me." She turned and looked thoughtful with her hand on her hip. "Uncle William, you were right about a Republican becoming the next president. How did you know?"

"Well, it only made sense to me after the mess that the Democrats got us into."

"I bet the Democrats don't see it that way, though. You'd probably have quite an argument." Melinda laughed softly. "When will McKinley be inaugurated?"

"March fourth. He'll be our twenty-fifth president."

Melinda set the table with a lacy tablecloth and as she got the plates out of the cupboard, Aunt Martha said, "Oh, I forgot to tell you. Put on two extra plates today. We're having company over."

Melinda smiled. Her aunt and uncle always seemed to find someone to invite over and they enjoyed sharing their food and charity with others.

"We've invited that nice young man and his daughter, Gilbert and Jenny."

Melinda froze. Her heart beat rapidly. She looked over at her aunt with widened eyes and asked, "Mr. Roberts and Jenny?"

Aunt Martha nodded. "I know they don't have kin close around here and I always like to invite them over whenever we have a special celebration."

Melinda quickly exited the room and ran upstairs to fix her hair. As she looked into the mirror and primped, she thought, "Why do I care what I look like? He's just Jenny's father. He's nothing to me."

She tried to ignore the fact that just recently her heart had seemed to flutter whenever Gilbert's name was mentioned at the table.

As she descended the stairs, she saw Gilbert already sitting on the sofa with Jenny. He stood politely as she walked into the room and he smiled with his hat in his hand.

Melinda nodded to them. "Mr. Roberts, Jenny."

"Please call me Gilbert. Mr. Roberts sounds so formal. May I call you Melinda?"

She smiled and nodded her assent.

"Melinda, how are you doing?" Gilbert asked with concern. "I haven't talked to you since the bear attack in October. I've seen you in town off and on, but we both seem to be in a hurry and don't take the time to visit. Are you doing all right?"

"Yes. It took a couple weeks to get over it. I would have nightmares each night and wake up in a cold sweat. I had to take the medicine the doctor gave me just before I went to bed so I could sleep. But I'm all right now. I'm sleeping much better. I have a lot to learn here in the West, don't I?" She smiled and gave a nervous sigh. "Thanks for asking."

Gilbert's heart felt heavy as he listened and knew that it must have been very difficult to overcome such a tremendous fright. He was surprised that she still acted positive about the West, though, and this made his admiration for her grow.

Jenny looked at her father and excitedly announced, "Did you know that the Pilgrims didn't eat what we're eating today, Pa?"

"No, I didn't, little darlin'."

Jenny blushed furiously and quickly leaned over to her father and whispered, "Pa! Don't call me that in front of company."

"Oh, I'm sorry, Jen," Gilbert said quietly while trying very hard to suppress a chuckle. "So, what did they eat?"

"Well, first, you have to know their celebration lasted for three days. At the feast they had dried fruit, berries, plums, ducks, fish, lob— lob— lob..." She looked up to her teacher with questioning eyes.

Melinda picked up her message immediately and continued, "Lobster, clams, and venison."

"Really?" Gilbert looked at Melinda with a smile. "I didn't know that."

Jenny was excited to tell her father a little more and continued, "Yes. The *Mayflower* arrived in America on December 11th in 1620 but it was real sad, Pa." Looking at her teacher for help, she said, "Tell him why, Miss Gamble."

Melinda looked at Gilbert and saw the interest in his eyes and said, "Well, their first winter was devastating because they lost 46 of the original 102. The Indians helped the Pilgrims survive the following year, so the remaining colonists decided to celebrate with a feast. There were ninety-one Indians who attended the celebration."

"You don't say!"

"Yes, Pa, it's true. We celebrate Thanksgiving because of President Lincoln. At first, George Washington wanted to make a National Day of Thanksgiving. That was in seventeen...uhm..."

Melinda interjected, "In 1789, but some were opposed to it."

"Opposed?" Gilbert looked at Melinda. He noticed how beautiful she looked and how her green eyes lit up as she spoke. "Why on earth would anyone oppose such a thing?"

"Well, they had their reasons. President Thomas Jefferson scoffed at the idea of having a day of thanksgiving. The idea brought a lot of discord among all the settlers because many felt that the hardships of just a few Pilgrims did not warrant a national holiday."

Gilbert's eyes widened. "Just a few Pilgrims? They sound a bit snooty to me."

"Yes, I think so, too. As Jenny was telling you, it wasn't until 1863 that President Lincoln proclaimed the last Thursday in November as a National Day of Thanksgiving."

Jenny's eyes lit up as she remembered more of what she had learned at school. "And it was all because of perse— perse—" She cleared her throat and blurted out, "Because of religion, Pa."

Melinda could not hold back and began to laugh softly. Jenny was trying so hard to remember what she had been taught at school. "What she's trying to say is that it all started because of religious persecution. The Pilgrims were Puritans and had fled their home in England to escape the persecution."

"Well, I'll be! A person can never stop learning no matter how old they are."

That made Jenny burst into laughter. Holding her sides with her hands, she giggled. After getting her breath back, she said, "I thought you knew everything, Pa."

"Not by a long shot!"

Melinda laughed and then excused herself to help Aunt Martha. She turned and walked into the kitchen to help her aunt put the food on the table. Aunt Martha looked over at her and smiled contentedly.

"Oh, Melinda dear, will you please go into the utility room and fill our large barrel up with plenty of water? I have a couple of buckets sitting beside the sink in there that you can use and I placed the barrel on the floor. I want us to bob for apples afterwards. It will be so much fun."

"I'd be glad to, Aunt Martha."

"Thanks, my dear. I appreciate it. If it weren't forty degrees outside, we'd go out there to do it. But..." She let her words trail off, busying herself again.

Melinda headed for the door that led into the utility room. It was the place where they did their wash, dried and bottled fruit, and washed vegetables from the garden.

When Gilbert saw her leave, he hopped up from the sofa. He had been watching her intently from the living room and heard what Aunt Martha had asked of Melinda. He thought he could help, so he nonchalantly walked past Martha and followed Melinda into the utility room.

Melinda looked up and saw him approaching while she was vigorously pumping the water into the first bucket. When she picked it up to move it out of the way, Gilbert appeared beside her and quickly took the full bucket of water from her hand. The sudden movement jolted the bucket and made the water slosh over the edge and onto Melinda's beautiful pink-flowered dress and upon her shoes, soaking her through from her waist to the floor.

Gilbert quickly jumped back as the water sloshed over the edges, so he would not get wet. Then looking at

Melinda's wet dress and shoes, he began to chuckle. It was quite a humorous situation. He had come out to help her but ended up spilling water all over her instead.

Melinda looked down at her dripping dress and wet shoes in despair and then looked up at Gilbert, who by now was laughing heartily.

With a combination of bewilderment and frustration, she asked, "What are you doing?"

He chuckled, "I thought I would come and help."

"Help?" The irritation in her voice was obvious. "You're laughing like a hyena. Look what you've done to my dress and shoes."

"It was an accident." Gilbert looked her up and down and tried to suppress another chuckle that wanted to burst through. "Did you think I had planned this whole thing so I could make you look silly? I must seem like a very devious person to you."

His eyes were full of amusement as he grinned at her, trying with all his might to hold back another chuckle.

With an indignant tone, she answered, "No, I didn't think that at all. I just got impatient because you spilled water all over me and you didn't even say you were sorry. All you did was just stand there and laugh at me." She put her hands on her hips and shook her head. "How exasperating you are!"

As Gilbert emptied the rest of the water from the bucket into the barrel, Melinda began to fill the second bucket.

Gilbert was still chuckling as he said, "No, you are wrong there. I didn't laugh at *you*. I was laughing at the situation. I had come to help, and in helping I hadn't really helped at all, but made everything worse. Don't you see the humor in it?"

Melinda looked up at him and saw a grin on his face. She thought he had a very twisted sense of humor and all at her expense, too. Quickly she picked up the bucket and walked over to the barrel and poured the water in with a sober and irritated look on her face.

"Melinda, you are so independent. Why don't you just let me help you with the water? You could have been filling one bucket as I dumped the other. We could have gotten this whole business over with a lot faster if you hadn't stopped to get angry with me. Where's your sense of humor?"

Melinda glanced up at him and then turned away. "I have a sense of humor."

"Well, this situation would have been very funny if you would have stood back and looked at it from a distance."

She glanced at his cheerful face and ignored him. Then she went back to the sink and began to fill both buckets up once more.

Gilbert grinned at her stubborn attitude and asked, "Now may I help you with the buckets this time?"

After filling both buckets full of water and placing them on the floor, she put her hands on her hips and said in a sober tone, "Help yourself."

Gilbert could see that she was out of sorts with him and he needed to smooth things over. So he walked toward her, looked into her stubborn green eyes and then took her by the shoulders and said, "I'm sorry for laughing. Will you forgive me? That was rude of me and I should've apologized for spilling water all over your beautiful dress. You look real nice this afternoon and I spoiled it all. Please forgive me." When she didn't respond, he cleared his throat. "I'm sort of eating humble pie right now."

Melinda looked into his eyes and saw his pleading look. Then she gave a slight smile. "I do have a sense of humor. You just haven't seen it yet."

Gilbert smiled, dropped his hands from her shoulders and reached for the two buckets, heading for the barrel. Melinda looked down at her soaking wet dress and then turned on her heels and walked toward the door.

"I've got to get changed."

As Gilbert dumped the two buckets of water into the barrel, he watched her leave and thought, "I've never met a more independent and stubborn woman! We're as different as night and day."

As Melinda passed Aunt Martha, she noticed a questioning look on Martha's face as she saw her dress. Before Martha could say a word, she said, "Don't ask, Aunt Martha."

After everyone was seated, Uncle William said the prayer. Then he looked around the table and said, "Before we eat, we have a tradition in our family. We all say something that we are thankful for. All right, I'll begin. I'm thankful for my sweet wife and that she puts up with me no matter how ornery I get." He looked over at Martha and smiled. "I love you, dear."

Melinda noticed the love that her aunt and uncle had for one another and it touched her heart. Aunt Martha was next.

"I'm thankful for you, too, dear. And I'm thankful for the nice fire that makes us feel cozy and warm and for this food that we can share with others."

Melinda smiled and thought for a moment. Then she said, "I'm thankful for living in this beautiful land here. I'm thankful for nature, the birds and the lake, the mountains and streams, and my students." She smiled at Jenny.

It was Jenny's turn and she said, "I'm thankful for school and learning. I didn't know it could be so much fun to learn."

Gilbert was next. He hesitated. He looked around the table. Then he cleared his throat. "I'm thankful for many things. But, I'm especially thankful for new beginnings. When I lost my wife eight years ago, I thought my life was at an end. Then Jenny filled my life with joy and we had one another. She filled every need that I had. I had someone to take care of and someone to protect. This was all I needed, I thought. But, lately I've found that I can find room in my life for others, for all of you. And I never thought I would find room for anyone else. So, I'm thankful for new beginnings."

The room was quiet and everyone sat still thinking about what he had said.

Gilbert turned to William and asked, "May we eat now?"

Uncle William laughed and began carving the turkey while Aunt Martha passed the rolls, mashed potatoes, and relish around. After eating a hearty meal, Aunt Martha announced that everyone was going into the utility room to bob for apples.

Jenny laughed excitedly as she knelt on the floor. After several tries, she decided to try a new method. She searched for an apple that was just her size. Then with her teeth, she clamped down on the stem of the apple and pulled it out of the water.

Jenny took the apple out of her mouth and grinned. "That's how it's done." Everyone laughed at her ingenuity. "Miss Gamble, it's your turn now."

Melinda shook her head vigorously and said, "I've already gotten wet once today. No more!" Then she looked at Gilbert and he grinned.

"Pa, how about you?" Jenny said.

Gilbert smiled at his daughter and said, "All right, Jen. I'll show you how it's supposed to be done."

Gilbert knelt on the floor beside the barrel. Just before he stuck his face into the water, he grinned at Melinda as if he were a schoolboy getting ready to show off. He eyed the floating bright red apples that bobbed on the water and found one that appealed to him. Then guiding it to the edge of the barrel with his mouth and nose, he pressed the apple firmly against the wooden frame of the barrel. With this maneuver, he was able to sink his teeth into the flesh of the apple. After a short while, his face popped out of the water with the apple in his mouth. Everyone cheered as Martha handed him a towel to dry his dripping face and the spirit of happiness seemed to spread from one person to the next.

While everyone was cheering the difficult feat that he had accomplished, Melinda remembered the twinkle in his eyes and his smile just before he went after the apple and she wondered why he seemed so charming. He had a boyish sort of grin and he seemed so pleased when he came up out of the water with the apple in his mouth. When he grinned at her, it seemed to light up the atmosphere.

Melinda was not quite sure how she felt about Gilbert. All she knew was that he was a very good father and she seemed to be attracted to him, regardless of how exasperating he was at times.

Chapter 13
CHRISTMASTIME

The snow gracefully fell to the ground, upon Melinda's hair, and on her nose. She looked at the snow-capped mountains. Every cliff and valley was dotted with snow, accentuating the rugged mountains. The limbs of the pines seemed to be weighed down with snow and it sparkled in the glow of the sun. It was almost Christmas.

Melinda watched a playful kitten that was batting its paws at the fluffy flakes. She mischievously tapped the snow-capped branch, which disturbed the snow and a small amount tumbled to the ground. It startled the kitten and it arched its back and hissed at the clump of snow. Melinda laughed out loud as the hairs of the kitten stood on end. She stooped down and brushed the snow off the kitten, picked it up and cuddled it in her arms.

Melinda heard the clip-clopping of hooves and she immediately looked up and noticed Gilbert and Jenny reining in their horses.

Gilbert had a broad smile on his face and he seemed to be amused at Melinda's playful ways. He said softly, "Playful kitten."

Melinda had forgotten they had been invited over for supper that evening. Jenny slid off her horse and scooped up a handful of snow in her gloved hands. She padded it tightly and took aim.

"Pa, watch out."

Just as he looked toward her, the snowball hit him in the chest. Surprised, he quickly slid off his horse and grabbed a handful of snow and hid it behind his back.

Walking toward Jenny, he said, "So, Jenny. You want to play? You want a snowball fight, eh?"

Jenny smiled and nodded.

"All right, you asked for it."

Quickly he swung his arm forward and the snowball hit Jenny right on the chin.

Jenny was not ready for such a sneaky move and was startled. Then she burst into laughter, "Hey, Pa. That was fast thinking. I didn't even have time to duck."

Noticing a handful of snow in Jenny's hand, Gilbert warned, "Hey, Jen. If you want Saint Nicholas to visit you this Christmas, you'd better be good to your pa or a piece of coal may end up in your stocking this year."

Jenny laughed as she dropped the snowball on the ground. She understood her father's warning and he did not have to say more. They tied their horses to the hitching post and walked arm in arm toward Melinda. Melinda was laughing softly and smiling at the fun that a father and his daughter could have together.

As they sat around the kitchen table talking, Gilbert noticed the beautiful Christmas tree through the doorway. It was decorated in red and gold with a star on top. There was a wreath above the fireplace and a toy train had been placed around the tree for decoration. A few presents had been placed under the tree and just above the kitchen doorway was mistletoe for fun and tradition.

Gilbert grinned at the mistletoe and looked over at Melinda, but when his eyes met Aunt Martha's, she winked at him, which made him laugh. It was a low, pleasant sounding laugh and Melinda suddenly turned her head and looked at Gilbert in a questioning manner, but he only shrugged and smiled.

"So, where are you going for Christmas, Melinda?" he asked.

"Back to Boston. I leave tomorrow morning."

"That's near the ocean, isn't it?"

"Yes, the Atlantic."

"Do you get snow there?"

"Yes, but not like this. I've never seen such deep snow as this before. And the mountains? Goodness. We don't have mountains in Boston. There are beauties here that I never imagined."

Gilbert smiled. He loved this area, living in the Rocky Mountains. People called it the Wild West because it had not been tamed. But many moved to the West for peace of mind, away from the noises and humdrum of city life. There was something peaceful about the West, yet exciting at the same time. There was a touch of danger to those who were not used to the West, but they soon learned how to deal with it and what to watch out for. The rugged mountains were unique and magnificent. This valley had acres of farmland and the cattle seemed to thrive here. And if anyone needed to do any major shopping or desired to attend a nearby college, he or she could travel over the mountain to Logan, Utah. Paris was Gilbert's home and he was proud of it.

After supper was over, Melinda sat at the piano and played Christmas carols while everyone lounged in chairs. As they felt the spirit of Christmas, they began to sing one carol after another. After a while, Gilbert stood and walked over to the piano and watched Melinda's hands dance gracefully across the keys as he sang. His deep, rich baritone voice rang through the room and Melinda was very surprised that this rugged rancher had such a lovely voice. She was learning more about him each time he came over for Sunday dinner, which was nearly every week. For some reason, Aunt Martha had taken him under her wing and he was becoming a regular guest in the home.

When the song came to an end, she turned in her seat and looked up into his face. "You have a lovely voice."

Gilbert could see the surprise in her eyes and hear it in her voice. He raised his eyebrows and said jokingly, "Thanks. I sing to my cows so they'll give me more milk."

Melinda laughed softly at the thought of Gilbert singing to his cows. "Now that's something I would like to see."

Gilbert enjoyed her delightful laughter and noticed that her eyes seemed to glow with happiness. Her charm was like a fairy gift from angels. And she had an ethereal beauty about her that made it difficult to stop gazing at her. Was it because it was Christmas that made her seem more beautiful to him? Was it his imagination that she seemed more at ease around him or were they just getting to know one another better? He had noticed his attraction toward her was growing with each visit and he looked forward to every Sunday meal at Martha's home.

"Mr. Roberts, have you heard of 'Far, Far Away on Judea's Plains'?"

"Yes, I have."

"Did you know that it was composed by a Mormon pioneer from St. George, Utah?"

"Yes, I did."

Gilbert was amused that Melinda would underestimate his knowledge of music. He did not know the classical composers and music like Melinda did, but when it came to Christmas music he had no competition. Christmas was one of his favorite times of the year. He did know one classical composer, though, and that was Handel because he had written "Joy to the World."

"In fact, Melinda, I heard that John Macfarlane woke up in the middle of the night with the tune and words in his head. It was so strong that he couldn't go back to sleep, so he woke his wife up and asked her to help him. He lit a lantern and then began playing and singing the song that came from his heart while his sweet wife helped him write each note and word down on paper. They stayed up all night until they finished the song."

Melinda's eyes lit up. "I didn't know that."

"He died four years ago in 1892."

"I didn't know that, either." She smiled. "Do you want to sing it with me?"

Gilbert nodded and she turned back to the piano, flipped the page over, and began playing.

Gilbert's rich baritone voice blended beautifully with Melinda's mellow alto voice. The blend of harmony was so beautiful and each word was sung with such feeling that a hush came over the room as they sang.

Far, far away on Judea's plains,
Shepherds of old heard the joyous strains:
Glory to God, Glory to God,
Glory to God in the highest;
Peace on Earth, good-will to men;
Peace on Earth, good-will to men!

After they finished the song, the room was still and no one said a word. Melinda could feel the sweet spirit in the room and she turned to look at Gilbert. He had an air of joy and contentment about him and she wondered if he could feel the peaceful atmosphere in the room as she did.

When their eyes met, Melinda felt warmth creep into her cheeks. His eyes seemed to be searching hers. But why? Feeling uncomfortable, she quickly averted her eyes and stood.

"Jenny, I have a gift for you because I won't be here for Christmas to give it to you," Melinda said.

Melinda walked over to the Christmas tree, picked up a small gift, and handed it to Jenny and then sat down. Jenny's eyes sparkled with delight as she ripped the paper open. Before her eyes was a lovely blue ribbon.

"It's for your hair, Jenny. And it's your favorite color, too."

Jenny ran to Melinda and wrapped her arms around her neck, hugging her tightly. Melinda sighed and wrapped her arms around Jenny. Jenny's voice sounded constricted as she spoke, "Thank you, Miss Gamble." She looked up into Melinda's eyes and said lovingly, "I love you."

Melinda was touched. She had not expected this. In fact, she had not been ready for this sudden display of affection. She had never had a student tell her that before and her eyes moistened; her chest was tight with emotion. These were such simple words, yet they seemed to have an intense effect upon her.

Gilbert watched his daughter and Melinda. He saw how touched Melinda was by his daughter's affection and he saw his daughter's love for her teacher. No other teacher had ever affected his daughter like this before. In fact, no other teacher had ever cared enough to help his daughter in school before. Melinda, he knew, had done some good in his daughter's life. In fact, he felt that she had made a difference in his own life, too. He felt alive again, as he had never felt before.

Aunt Martha had watched Gilbert at Thanksgiving and noticed that he seemed to be quite interested in Melinda, so she had made sure he was invited over every Sunday evening for supper. The town called Martha "Cupid" because she enjoyed pairing people up. And that was true. Martha wanted others to have the joy and happiness she had in marriage. So, when she noticed Gilbert's interest in Melinda, she had decided on a plan.

While everyone had been singing, Martha had put a coffee table just inside the kitchen door, next to the doorway where the mistletoe hung. Then she carefully placed the dessert and plates upon it. When Melinda or Gilbert would get a cookie or brownie, they would be positioned perfectly under the mistletoe. Martha thought her idea was very clever.

Uncle William watched Martha studiously and he chuckled. He knew his wife and he knew what she was doing. He sat comfortably on the sofa as Martha came with a plate of cookies for him and for Jenny.

As she handed Jenny her plate, she said, "Sit by the fire and enjoy the warmth while you eat your dessert."

Then she sat down beside William and handed him his plate with a smile. William whispered in her ear, "Thanks, Cupid."

Aunt Martha acted innocent. "What do you mean?"

Uncle William whispered, "I've been living with you for over fifty years now and I believe I know you inside and out."

He grinned at her as she tried to act innocent and then he kissed her cheek lovingly.

Ignoring his astuteness, Aunt Martha called out, "Dessert everyone! There's cookies, brownies, and tarts on the coffee table."

Melinda headed for the dessert table and began filling a plate. As she stood in the doorway of the kitchen, it had not dawned on her why Aunt Martha had put the table there instead of the living room. Gilbert walked up to the coffee table, waiting for his turn. He had noticed the mistletoe, but was not sure if he should say anything or if he should take advantage of the situation.

Martha grinned and said, "Oh, oh. Look at that. Melinda is under the mistletoe. Well, what are you going to do about it, Gilbert? You can't let her get away tomorrow on that train without a kiss, especially when it's tradition. No one can avoid the mistletoe, you know."

Melinda quickly looked up at the mistletoe in surprise and then jerked her head toward Aunt Martha with a shocked, knowing expression.

When she turned to face Gilbert, his soft eyes seemed to glow as he stood before her. Melinda quickly touched her cheek with the tips of her fingers when she felt the warmth creep into her face. She felt so embarrassed. She was nervous and felt uneasy as he gazed into her eyes. She was not sure what to expect.

Gilbert smiled with amusement when he saw her blush a rosy color, and he said in a low and soft tone, "Melinda?"

His eyes held hers as he searched them for an answer. Then Melinda lowered her eyelids and looked down at her hands that were nervously playing with the red satin ribbon at her waist. Gilbert could see that she felt apprehensive and uneasy and he did not want to embarrass her more than she already was. So, as his eyes stayed glued to her expression, he gently took her slender hand into his and lifted it toward his lips. Then he pressed them tenderly against the back of her hand, lingering a bit.

Melinda was surprised at this chivalrous gesture and raised her eyes to meet his. The tenderness of his kiss and the softness in his eyes touched Melinda and a warm glow filled her soul. She was sure he could feel her pulse race as he held her hand in his and her fingers seemed to tingle from the touch of his lips. It did not take much to turn her face a rosy glow once again. Then, instantly, a strange sensation of joy came over her that she had not expected.

Gilbert let go of her hand as he turned to Aunt Martha and said, "We had better go, Martha. It's getting late."

The softness of Melinda's hand in his and her many blushes seemed to have their effects on Gilbert. His heart had skipped a beat that night and he felt it was time to leave. He was not ready for what his heart was trying to tell him. He had concerns that he was not yet ready to face.

Aunt Martha grabbed their coats and a bag with cookies and roast beef inside and handed them to Gilbert. As she walked them to the door, she whispered, "Don't worry. She'll soften towards you. It will just take time."

After they left, Melinda felt as if she were in a daze as she walked upstairs to her bedroom. Her heart was full and she didn't know why. For the life of her, she could not figure out why she had reacted in such a way to his tenderness. She tried not to think about it because the following day she would be catching the train to Boston and she needed her sleep.

Chapter 14
CHRISTMAS VACATION

As the train clattered down the tracks, Melinda was thinking of home. She could not wait to see her parents. She pictured her mother's face. Her hair was slightly graying, but she still had a youthful look. Her father was a tall, heavy man who spent too many days at his desk. He never found time to exercise, so he tended to be overweight. He had a thick salt-and-pepper mustache and a large, rounded nose. Melinda felt that there was more of him to love than an ordinary father and loved him just the way he was. She would not change one thing about him.

Melinda had fond memories of vacationing with her parents. The bond between them was solid. Her memory went back to ten months ago when her father had excitedly bought the three of them tickets for the grand opening of the Crystal Carnival and Ice Palace in Leadville, Colorado.

When she had looked upon the Ice Palace from a distance, it had seemed like a fairyland. As the three of them approached the Ice Palace, she was in awe. It glimmered with the sun's glow and her heart beat rapidly with excitement. It was made of five thousand tons of ice blocks formed into the shape of a magnificent palace, measuring 325 feet by 180 feet with towers reaching 90 feet high by 40 feet wide, and it enclosed five acres of ground.

This Ice Palace reminded her of the fairy tales of Cinderella and Sleeping Beauty. It sparkled and glimmered in the sun and she felt like a princess walking into a storybook world.

Her father had put his arm around her shoulders and said, "When you were a little girl, did you picture the palaces of kings and queens to look like this?"

The three of them walked together arm in arm into this magnificent man-made creation. Inside the palace, there was a dance floor, a restaurant, a gaming room, and a 180-foot ice rink. It was illuminated with electric lights that sparkled against the ice blocks.

She remembered how her father had danced with her mother on the dance floor of this Ice Palace and how lovingly he had held her in his arms. Her father was deeply in love with her mother and Melinda longed for a marriage such as they had: one of equality, where the man respected the woman and supported her education. Her father had never taken her mother for granted and he worked alongside her when it came to household chores. Would she ever find a man like her father? she wondered.

Then her thoughts turned to Gilbert. Would he treat her in such a loving manner? Would he respect her and treat her as an equal? Or would he be opinionated and stubborn, and refuse to share in the chores? He did know how to cook, however. That was one point on his side. But on the other hand, he certainly had been stubborn that first day they met. Melinda laughed as she remembered the little arguments they had had and when he had called her "self-willed." She hated that word, but she knew it was true. Melinda quickly shook the memory of him out of her mind. No, they were much too different. It simply would not work.

Just then the train pulled to a stop and she saw her father and mother waiting for her with smiling faces. As soon as she stepped off the train, she leaped into their arms. Tears were shed and hugs were exchanged and all the way back home there was constant chatter.

That evening, as soon as she got settled down, she walked down the staircase to the living room and she found James waiting for her.

"Melinda, you look even more lovely than I remember."

James took her hand in his and kissed it tenderly. Melinda noticed that she did not respond the same way to James as she had to Gilbert's kiss. Her heart did not flutter and her hand did not tingle from the softness of his lips.

Her mother walked in with a smile on her face. "I invited James over for dinner. I thought the two of you could catch up on old times."

Melinda smiled. Her mother and Aunt Martha had so much in common. They were both matchmakers. Melinda knew that her mother wanted her to marry James, but she couldn't help but wish they would both relax and let her make up her own mind.

James was a good man and they had much in common, but she didn't love him. He did not make her heartbeat quicken; he did not make her blush at the thought of him. When James kissed her hand, it felt like nothing more than the kiss of an old friend, but James did not seem to realize that.

On the other hand, Gilbert and she were as different as night and day, and yet she felt attracted to him. Why? She remembered his lingering kiss and how warm and tender it had been. The memory of it seemed to linger in her mind. Her heart had raced when he had touched her hand and when he kissed it, and a tingling sensation seemed to start at her knuckles and make its way to her heart. As she thought of Gilbert and her last night with him, a tingle of excitement went through her and she smiled.

After dinner, she and James made plans to go to Tchaikovsky's Nutcracker Ballet. "It's a new ballet," James told her. "Only three years old. I know you'll enjoy it. Then I'll take you to the Messiah on Christmas Eve."

James spoiled her each day and the week passed quickly and soon it was Christmas Eve. James arrived to pick her up and was waiting in the living room for her. When he saw her descend the stairs, his eyes happily swept over her.

Melinda was dressed in an elegant silk violet gown with sleeves that were gathered at the shoulders and hung freely to her elbows. Her hair was secured loosely upon her head with silver combs.

James looked into her eyes and smiled. "You look absolutely lovely tonight, Melinda."

Melinda smiled in a coy manner. "Why, thank you, James."

James took her by the arm and walked her toward the carriage. The carriage ride was pleasant and she enjoyed seeing her hometown once again. Melinda had many lovely memories growing up here and joy filled her soul as she looked around at the scenery. It did not take long before they arrived at the concert hall.

James held his hand out to help her down from the carriage and they walked into the building arm in arm. Upon entering the hall, Melinda noticed three gigantic chandeliers that glimmered and sparkled from the light in the room. People were dressed elegantly and bustling about.

They found seats in the auditorium and sat whispering together until the performance was ready to begin. James told her of all the success he was having as a lawyer, how much he wished that she would come back home to stay, and bragging about how important she would be if she married him.

The performance began and all was quiet. As they sat listening to the magnificent music of Handel, James leaned over and whispered, "I bet they don't have this type of entertainment in the Wild West." Then he chuckled softly as if the West were a big joke to him.

As the choir sang, the rich voices filled the concert hall. Melinda's heart was touched when they sang the "Hallelujah Chorus." Everyone in the audience stood out of respect for the song. Her eyes filled with tears because of the beauty of that magnificent song and its message, and a reverence filled her soul.

When the concert had finished, Melinda took James's arm and walked toward the carriage in silence. The memory of those songs lingered within her as she stepped into the carriage. As they headed home, James broke the silence.

"I enjoyed being with you tonight. I can see that you really enjoyed the concert, too. You must have missed the East with all its balls, concerts, ballets, and parties. The West doesn't have the sophistication that the East has. The West is no place for a lady like you, Melinda. Stay here. Marry me. And you will never have to work again."

Melinda looked into his eyes. "James, you don't understand. No, the West doesn't have the concerts and ballets that you have here, but it has something the East doesn't have. It has heart. It has no pretense. You know where you stand with people out there and you don't have to put on a show as you do here with all your fancy gowns and finery, trying to outdo one another. And about working...you don't seem to understand that I love it. Of course, it isn't easy and I get frustrated at times, but it's all worth it. Those children need me. And besides, I love them dearly."

"But Melinda, it's about time that you settled down and had a family of your own."

Trying to remain calm, she answered with a bit of frustration, "James, I'm tired of men who don't believe women can do more with their lives. Yes, I want a family. I want a family very much, but the only words that seem to come out of your mouth are about me forsaking my job and marrying you so that I can wait on you hand and foot."

James's eyes widened at that statement. "I didn't say anything about you waiting on me. Although it doesn't sound like a bad idea. I'd like to be spoiled by a woman. Doesn't any man?"

Melinda shook her head in frustration. "Take me home. I don't want to discuss this any longer."

James looked into Melinda's eyes, trying to understand her. He looked confused. Then, as if to persuade her through what he perceived to be of interest to all women, he changed the subject to shopping.

"How you can stand such an uncivilized world is beyond me!" he exclaimed. "They don't have the shopping stores and the social life we have here. If you marry me, I'll buy you whatever your little heart desires."

Melinda shook her head. "I can't. I don't love you, James. I told you that before I left."

The carriage stopped in front of her home and James once again put his hand out to help her out of the carriage. Then he smiled and said, "Well, I still have a week to convince you until you go back."

Melinda grinned and decided to forgive his inability to understand her. "You're incorrigible, James."

"I know. And I'm not giving up until you're on that train heading west."

Melinda smiled as he took her hand and led her to the front door.

Chapter 15
THE NEW YEAR'S EVE PARTY

The rest of the week went by much more quickly than she realized, and before she knew it Melinda was packing to leave for the West. After she packed, she hurriedly dressed for the New Year's Eve party. She wore an embroidered light green muslin dress that her mother had made as a Christmas gift. It fit her figure perfectly and hung gracefully about her feet. The neckline was squared and the puffed sleeves were gathered at the elbow. Her dress brought out the green in her eyes and she was happier than usual that evening, not for the fact that she was going to the New Year's Eve dance, but because she was returning to her second home in the morning.

As she walked down the stairs, James was waiting. He gave her a hug and said, "Melinda, you look lovely. I'll be the envy of every gentleman tonight."

He escorted her to the carriage and they talked all the way to the dance. As they entered the party, Melinda saw a few of her friends and they had a brief visit before James escorted her onto the dance floor. She spent most of the dances that night with James and several friends whom she had not seen for months before she stopped to rest.

While conversing with her friends, one young woman inquired with derisive laughter, "Well, what's the Wild West like, Melinda? How can you stand being away from society that long?"

Melinda did not comment because the rest of her friends roared in laughter. Nothing she could say would make her friends understand the peace and tranquility she felt among the mountains and the countryside.

Melinda looked around at everyone. The room was a clamor of noise and the people were bustling about. Women were flirtatious with anyone who noticed. Men responded with insincerity. Both men and women had drinks in their hands and acted as if there were no tomorrow and they did not care about anything but the moment. And especially on this night, fidelity and respect did not seem important to anyone. To these people, money was important. Women sat admiring one another's dress and waving their fans in the air with feigned sophistication, batting their eyes at anyone who was male.

There seemed to be such worldliness in the air and it bothered Melinda. She neither smoked nor drank and she had high standards—among them, fidelity towards one's spouse. These beliefs were part of her upbringing and religion and she practiced them faithfully.

When the New Year's chimes rang, they all cheered and threw their hats in the air and blew their horns while music played on stage. James grabbed Melinda and kissed her.

"Happy New Year, sweetheart." Then he went down the line kissing a few more friends in a most jovial manner.

Melinda felt numb from all the cacophony of noise in the room. She felt out of place. She had been to New Year's Eve parties before, so why was this year so different to her? As she stood in thought, she wondered how those in Bear Lake were celebrating. Her thoughts began to stray to Uncle William and Aunt Martha and she wondered how they celebrated the New Year. Then her mind wandered to Gilbert and Jenny and she wondered how they were celebrating.

Meanwhile, back in Bear Lake Valley, folks were celebrating the New Year in a completely different manner. Uncle William and Aunt Martha were celebrating with a few friends they had invited over, playing games and singing songs. Someone played the piano while others snacked on goodies that Martha had made. Her friends had brought treats from their own homes as well. When the New Year rang in, Uncle William and Aunt Martha kissed tenderly and then everyone hugged. Afterwards they took pots and pans and went outside and banged them loudly with a ladle, yelling to all the neighbors, "Happy New Year. Happy New Year to everyone!"

Gilbert and Jenny celebrated a little differently. They sat together at the table playing checkers, hand games, and card games, laughing each time someone would win.

"How about an arm wrestle, Pa? I've been workin' extra hard lately and I think that I'm up to it now."

Gilbert grinned at his daughter's confidence. "Sure. Let's have a try at it. But I have to warn you, I feel mighty strong tonight, Jen."

"You sure sound confident, Pa. Now don't get a big head or I'll have to whop you at arm wrestlin' to humble you a bit."

Gilbert chuckled as he clasped Jenny's hand firmly and grinned. She was sounding mighty grown up for an eight-year-old girl.

"Ready, Jen?"

"Ready."

Jenny pulled with all her might, squinting her eyes and pursing her lips together in concentration. Gilbert allowed his arm to be pulled back a bit and exclaimed, "Oh, no."

Then he pulled hers in his direction and watched her trembling arm as she pulled with all her might. Her face reddened with exertion as she struggled to pull her father's hand. The knuckles of her fingers turned white as she struggled to keep her arm from collapsing. After a while Gilbert began to moan and then he weakened his grip, which gave Jenny leverage, and she gradually pulled her father's arm toward her side. When she had him two inches from the table, he gave a slight groan and then gave a strong pull and brought her arm into an upright position once again. Jenny grunted and her arm began to quiver as she pulled with all her strength. Gilbert allowed Jenny to gradually pull his arm one inch from the table. After struggling for a minute and watching Jenny's trembling arm and tightened muscles in her face, he allowed his arm to be pulled to the table.

With a whoop and a holler, she jumped from the table with joy. "I did it! I did it! That's my first time to ever…" she stopped in mid sentence and peered into Gilbert's face. "Pa, you cheated."

"No, I didn't, Jen."

"Yes, you did. You cheated. You let me win on purpose."

"No, Jen. You won fair and square."

She shook her head vigorously and grinned, "I know you, Pa. You were feelin' sorry for me because I've never won yet and you just let me win. Confess, now."

"I'm confessing nothing to you, Jen," he said with a teasing glint in his eyes.

"Admit it, Pa. I can read the expression on your face. You can't hide it from me."

Gilbert guffawed as he held both hands up in surrender. "All right, I admit that I let you win and I promise you that it won't ever happen again. But if you want to know, you're getting mighty strong, young lady. And I had to struggle a bit."

Jenny giggled at his statement. "If that's supposed to make me feel better, it don't, Pa. One of these days I'll win at arm wrestlin'. You just wait and see."

"That's a deal," Gilbert chuckled between his words.

While Jenny set up another game, Gilbert stood and walked into the kitchen to get some treats to eat. Throughout the evening, they ate a few snacks that had been prepared along with cookies and punch. Gilbert read a few nonsensical poems by Lewis Carroll and made Jenny laugh until her sides ached. When they noticed the time, they both started the countdown, "Ten, nine, eight…"

When the New Year rang in, Jenny hugged her father and they danced together, singing a jovial song. Their voices rang with happiness with each melodic note. After they finished the song, they took a glass of punch and gave a toast to the New Year.

Gilbert smiled at his daughter and said, "May this year be better than last year and may we grow and learn from our mistakes."

Jenny added. "And I'm gonna try to be a better student for my teacher, Pa."

Gilbert smiled. "That was a good toast, Jenny."

They each took a sip of punch.

"I miss her, Pa." She lifted her eyebrows curiously. "Do you like Miss Gamble?"

Gilbert thought a while and nodded. "Yes, I do, Jenny."

"Pa, do you ever think you'll get married again?"

"Never really thought much about it."

"Why not, Pa?"

"Never saw a real need before."

"Why not, Pa?"

"I suspect that I've been so happy with my daughter and so busy on the ranch that I never really thought about it before."

"Pa, do you think you might start thinkin' about it now?"

Gilbert thought for a bit, rubbing his chin. "Perhaps. Why are you asking me all these questions, Jenny?"

"Just curious, that's all." She looked down at her feet and wiggled her toes. "I really like Miss Gamble, Pa."

Gilbert smiled. "Are all these questions that you've been asking me pointing to someone special, Jenny?"

"Perhaps."

Gilbert laughed. "You're just like your Pa. I say 'perhaps' just to avoid an answer and so do you."

Jenny giggled and Gilbert chuckled warmly. "Jenny, it's time for bed. Good night and I love you, dear. Sleep well."

After Jenny hugged her father and went to bed, he stayed up for a while thinking about what Jenny had said. Gilbert had been thinking about Melinda during the holidays and had missed her. He had been invited over to Martha's for Sunday dinners ever since Thanksgiving and he had become comfortable with Melinda and her ways. His thoughts would roam to their conversations and her beautiful green eyes and graceful movements. He knew that Jenny wanted a mother, but he was not quite ready for that commitment as of yet. He needed to guard his heart carefully because he had something that he needed to work out on his own before pursuing that direction.

Chapter 16
MELINDA'S SURPRISE

As the train pulled into Bear Lake Valley, Melinda felt like she was home again. After just four months, this place felt like home. Why was that? As she realized how special this quaint little town had become, her heart began to beat rapidly. She was excited to be home again. The mountains were covered with a white blanket and the land was knee-deep with snow. The green pines were dabbed with an icy crust and moved gently in the breeze.

The train slowed down as it approached the terminal. Melinda looked out the window, searching for her uncle and aunt. Her heart fluttered with excitement when she saw their carriage waiting for her. When the train came to a stop, she grabbed her two bags and purse. As she stepped to the edge of the passenger car, she breathed in the fresh crisp air and joy filled her heart. It smelled so clean and fresh, so different from the city.

Just as she began to step down, she heard a familiar voice. "May I take your luggage for you?"

Melinda recognized that voice and she immediately raised her head. There was Gilbert watching her descend the stairs. With surprise in her voice, she said, "Mr. Roberts?"

Gilbert was looking at her with interest. He hadn't seen her for a couple of weeks and he thought she looked mighty fine. "Martha asked me to pick you up. Your uncle is sick and she hated to leave him. She asked me to pick you up in her carriage because my buckboard wouldn't be as comfortable."

Gilbert held his hand out for her luggage and Melinda handed it to him. "May I take the other one, too?"

Melinda shook her head. "No, it's all right. I can manage. I don't want you to be weighed down when I'm perfectly able to carry at least one."

Gilbert chuckled at her independence. As she held her skirts and stepped down from the train, he watched her and said, "My, it's good to see you again."

Melinda was surprised to hear that. As she searched his eyes for a clue to his feelings, she asked, "It is? Why is that?"

Gilbert was not ready for that sort of question. He could not say exactly why he was so happy to see her. Could it have been that he had missed her and had been thinking about her for the past few weeks? He was not even sure of his own feelings at that moment. He was too concerned about the differences in their personalities.

"It just is," he blurted out.

"Oh." Melinda felt a little disappointed. She wondered if he had been thinking about her as much as she had about him. Slowly, they walked toward the carriage. "It's good to see you again, also."

Gilbert grinned as he began putting the luggage in the carriage. With a teasing tone in his voice, he asked, "It is? Why is that?"

When she saw him grin, she thought he seemed a little arrogant. Besides, she knew he was teasing her and she was not in the mood to be teased. Melinda noticed that he had not responded to her question, so why should she answer his? Two could play that game. No, she was not about to back down and dodge his question just as he had done, so she answered with a bluntness that surprised him.

"It's good to see you because I've been thinking about you. I wondered how your Christmas and New Year's Eve were. We're friends and I enjoy being around you. That's why. At least I can answer your question, which is more than you did." She looked into his eyes and added with a little impatience, "What are you so afraid of, Mr. Roberts?"

Melinda was not about to be intimidated by his question. She gave her answer and it was the truth, and she was proud of herself for not backing down. She watched Gilbert's face and waited patiently for his reaction.

When Gilbert heard her indignant tone, he grinned and then he burst out with laughter. "You know, Melinda, when we get together, we are just like two bulls butting heads."

Melinda was not sure if she liked that analogy, but she grinned and then laughed herself. "I guess we are. But I'm not quite sure that I like being compared to a bull. Do you really want to know how I feel?"

Gilbert nodded. He searched her face and eyes while he listened to her.

She continued, "You are so exasperating at times, Mr. Roberts, and I'm just not sure why. Maybe it's because you don't seem to show your feelings or even say what you feel. You seem to hide your emotions, and I don't know whether you like me or not. I simply asked you why it was good to see me, and you avoided the subject like an illness. I just don't understand you at all, Mr. Roberts."

She put her hands on her hips and stood looking at him impatiently, waiting for a response. She had been blunt and she wondered how he would take such an answer from a woman.

Melinda's words seemed to stir his heart. She cared. She actually cared. As she spoke, his eyes swept over her and he realized how attractive she was, even with all that spunk. Her auburn hair shone in the sun, and her rosy cheeks, her expressive green eyes, and the soft, gentle curves of her body made her look achingly beautiful to Gilbert. When his eyes strayed to the soft curvature of her mouth, a longing to kiss her rose sharply within him. Looking into her eyes and studying her intently, Gilbert impulsively stepped toward her and slid his hands around her waist, pulling her close to him, and pressed his warm lips to hers. Then he wrapped his arms around her and held her tenderly as his lips caressed hers. Relishing her softness in his arms, he let his kiss linger.

Melinda's heart began to beat rapidly and her pulse raced as it had never done before. His lips were warm and tender, and happiness overtook her, along with surprise. His hands were strong and his touch made her heart sing.

As he enfolded her in his arms and pulled her closer to his chest with the palms of his hands on her back, Melinda felt as if she were melting into his arms and a tingling sensation seemed to start from her lips and continue down to her toes. As she felt his muscled arms tighten around her in an embrace, she realized that she had never felt this way with any man before. Her spirits soared as happiness spread through her body and she found it difficult to come back to earth again. She felt him squeeze her tightly as his warm lips pressed against hers and she sighed in ecstasy. When he pulled away, she looked into his softened eyes and joy filled her soul.

Melinda's reception of his kiss had had its effect on Gilbert and he was not ready for what his heart was telling him. She seemed so vulnerable and he was afraid of hurting her. When Gilbert noticed how she had responded to his embrace and melted into his arms, he suddenly became unsure of himself. His heart had skipped several beats during that embrace and he had found it difficult to let her go. He knew that he had fallen in love with Melinda, but he needed time to think.

Gilbert looked into her eyes and said softly, "Melinda, I should take you home."

As he helped her into the carriage, his pulse was still racing and he tried to think of something to say. Should he have apologized for his behavior? Why had he acted so impulsively?

After climbing into the carriage, Gilbert whipped the reins and sat silently in thought, though very aware of Melinda sitting next to him. After a while, he decided to express a few of his concerns out loud.

"Melinda, we are so different, you and I. You're a lady of the best kind. I'm just a rancher, a cowpuncher, and you're a lady of the East. You're not used to this kind of life here. There's no future for us. Don't you see?"

Melinda could see the frustration in his face as she watched him speak. "No, Gilbert, you are wrong. I'm a lady of the West now. And you are much more than just a rancher. You don't see yourself as I do. You're a loving father, a devoted friend, a fantastic cook, a righteous man, and a protector. I feel that this land is mine now. I love it beyond words. I belong here and I know it."

Gilbert smiled. This was the first time she had called him by his given name. He had asked her to call him that twice before, but he had yet to hear it until now. He shook his head in dismay as he realized that even that was affecting his senses.

The trip home was quiet and peaceful. Melinda did not have much to say because her heart was still pounding with anxiety. She could still feel the taste of his kiss on her lips. Gilbert's kiss and his strong arms around her seemed to linger in her memory during the ride home, and she was very aware of her own feelings for the man sitting beside her.

Gilbert was quiet. He was wrestling with something very personal, something beyond what he had just revealed to her. His anguish was apparent and Melinda could see it clearly and wished that she could help in some way.

After he reined in the horse, he took her hand in his to help her down. He noticed how she gathered her skirts in her hand and gracefully stepped down from the carriage. Not wanting to let go, his hand lingered a while before releasing hers as he gazed deeply into her eyes, as if searching for a reason why he was feeling this way.

One question after another seemed to haunt him. What was it about Melinda that attracted him so? Was he actually in love for the first time in eight years? Why did they have to be so different? Why did he have to meet her and fall in love? He had not expressed all of his concerns to her, but at least he was able to express one of them.

After releasing her hand, Gilbert took her luggage to the door and placed them inside the house. He wanted to speak to her, but the words would not come.

Melinda said softly, "You needn't worry about the horse and buggy. I can unhitch the horse and put him away. I've been doing it for the past four months now. I'm capable."

A frown appeared upon his face and without a word, he abruptly turned around and walked toward the buggy and led the horse to the small barn. Gilbert unhitched the horse and put it in the stall. He was not about to let Melinda unhitch the buggy, no matter how independent she was. This was the least he could do for her. After shutting the gate, he took off toward his horse, which had been tied up to a hitching post near the house. Taking the reins in his hands, he climbed upon his horse and galloped away without looking back.

As Melinda watched from the doorway, she wondered what had just happened. Why had he been so abrupt when he left? Why didn't he allow her to unhitch the horse and buggy? Was something bothering him? And why didn't he look back at her before he left, as a friendly gesture? As she contemplated her own concerns, she realized that when he had pulled her into his arms, she had never felt warmer than at that very moment.

Chapter 17
THE BLIZZARD

A couple of weeks passed and Melinda had not had a chance to talk to Gilbert since he had kissed her at the train station. She had seen him a few times in town and he would nod and smile cordially at her, but he didn't go out of his way to make conversation with her.

Melinda thought about him often and tried to figure out her own feelings. The memory of his kiss and his embrace seemed to linger in her memory. At long last, she came to the conclusion that she must be in love with him. Why else would she have thought of him so often during her vacation? Why else would she have compared everything he did to James while she was back East? Why did a warm glow fill her heart whenever she thought about him? She had never felt this way when she was with James. Her thoughts seemed to stray toward Gilbert every waking moment. This had to be love. What else could it be?

Melinda awoke to howling winds. She stretched and then hopped out of bed. As she opened the curtains to her bedroom window, she was absolutely surprised at what she saw. Snowdrifts were up to the tops of the windows at the main level of the house. The wind was howling like a mad demon. She had never heard wind like this before and snow was pelting down toward her window so thick and large that she could not even see more than eight feet in front of her.

When she heard a yell of agony downstairs. Melinda grabbed a robe and ran downstairs to find Aunt Martha stepping into the house, holding Uncle William's arm around her shoulders.

"He's been hurt," Martha cried. "He just fed the horse and was coming in when he slipped on the icy steps. I think he's broken his ankle because he can't put any weight on it at all."

"Shall I get the doctor, Aunt Martha?"

"Yes, dear. Quickly."

"What about school and the children? They won't know what to do since I will be late."

Aunt Martha gently helped William down on the sofa and then looked at Melinda. "Oh, dear sweet Melinda. This is a blizzard. The children won't be going to school today. In fact, most people will be staying home if they have any sense at all. But there will be those merchants who feel the need to open their stores, which surprises me because who would want to go out in this weather to buy something?"

"Aunt Martha, I will hurry as quickly as I can. Don't worry. The doctor will be here soon."

"You'll have to walk, dear. If you take the carriage, this wind might tip you over and you'll get hurt. The wind is too powerful for that carriage. It's too lightweight and in no time the wind will have it toppled on its side."

"All right, Aunt Martha. I'll hurry."

Melinda remembered when she was seventeen years of age and the "Great White Hurricane" had paralyzed the East Coast. In 1888, a blizzard hit the coast that was stronger than anyone had expected. The telegraph and telephone wires had snapped, isolating New York, Boston, Philadelphia, and Washington, D.C., for days. Two hundred ships were grounded, and at least 100 seamen died. Fires broke out that were caused by the strong winds, and fire stations were immobilized. Because fire engines were not able to run, property loss from fire alone was estimated at $25 million. Temperatures plunged lower than anyone expected, and the ferocious wind continued for the next thirty-six hours. They estimated that fifty inches of snow fell in Connecticut and Massachusetts and forty inches covered New York and New Jersey. Winds blew up to forty-eight miles an hour, creating snowdrifts forty to fifty feet high. Overall, more than 400 deaths were reported on the East Coast. Because of the transportation crisis, this led to the creation of the New York subway, which was approved in 1894.

Without breakfast and without a word of farewell, Melinda dressed quickly and headed toward the door. As she tried to open it, the wind fought against her and she tugged and pulled on the door to open it. As she stepped out of the door, an icy blast of wind greeted her. Melinda pulled her woolen wrap around her head and neck and trudged through the blizzard.

The road was icy, but she stepped with firmness so her feet would not come out from beneath her. The wind blew so hard that she could barely keep her footing. Once she lost her balance, but she regained it quickly. As she leaned into the wind, she trudged forward, breathing heavily as she fought with the wind.

Melinda stopped to get her breath and held onto a tree to rest. She cupped her hands next to her face and her breath formed a small cloud around her mouth and nose as she warmed her face, but as quickly as it formed, the clouds of her breath whipped away instantly with the wind.

Her muscles ached from struggling with the mighty wind and her heart pounded furiously. She looked around, trying to get her bearings, and noticed a fallen tree on the side of the road. The snow was violently whirling around the tree and a snow bank was blocking her path.

Fighting the wind, she edged around the snow bank. Her cheeks and nose were stinging from the cold. Before she left, her aunt had told her that it was ten degrees outside without the wind factor. The biting wind seemed to nip at her nose and she rubbed it with her gloved hand. Pulling her wrap even tighter around her neck, she continued on her way.

The howling wind pushed against her, struggling to lift her from the ground. She passed three people who were clinging to one another as they headed home. She dodged debris that flew past her, rolling and tumbling down the street. A carriage was lying on its side and the owner was hunched over, fighting against the wind, as he led his horse down the street. A woman, her scarf and heavy coat crusted with snow and ice, struggled in the wind and eventually slipped to the ground, landing on her backside. A man, grasping his hat tightly with one hand and shielding his eyes with the other, saw her fall. He came running to her aid, but as he knelt beside her, his hat flew from his head and rose into the air, twirling and whirling around mounds of snow, and then gradually disappearing with the wind. Melinda noticed that his mustache was crusted with snow. A couple of young men passed her on snowshoes and called out to her, "This is no time to be out in this blizzard. Are you crazy, lady? You had better get home."

As she plodded forward, Melinda noticed how the mounds against the homes had drifted twenty feet high. She noticed how the ice had created white lace on the window-panes and for an instant she thought how beautiful it looked. After a while, she stopped beside a tree and held onto the trunk as she took a breath and looked around. She felt lost and confused. Everything seemed to be foreign to her. The snow was coming down so hard that she did not recognize where she was.

The wind howled ferociously and a blast of it struck her in the face. Melinda shivered and hugged herself with her arms to keep warm. The cold seemed to be penetrating through her woolen wrap and many petticoats, which were caked with snow and ice. She had hoped that her petticoats would her keep warm, but apparently it wasn't enough.

She took another step forward and the snow swallowed her from toes to knees. She found it difficult to move her feet, but she persisted and was able to pull herself out of the drifted snow. Her frozen face stung as the wind whipped around her. As she staggered against the wind, she fell into another snowdrift. Melinda had been out in this freezing weather too long and her senses were no longer clear. She could not think or walk normally. What was happening to her? Where were her senses? Why was her mind so foggy and why couldn't she walk with the same strength as before?

As she struggled to pick herself up, she heard a buckboard pulling up beside her. A deep voice called out to her with concern, "Hey, ma'am. This is no time to be out in this storm. You had better go home. Do you live very far from here?"

Holding her wrap closely around her face, she shivered and stuttered as she said, "S-sir, I'm headed for the doctor. M-my Uncle William has been hurt b-badly, but I've lost my way. I can't s-seem to get my b-bearings with all this s-snow coming down so thick around me."

"Melinda, is that you?"

Quickly, Gilbert hopped down from the buckboard and pulled the wrap away from her face. Her face was bright red and she was shivering uncontrollably. His eyes widened with shock as he saw her condition. "I'm taking my hired hand back home, but I can't leave you like this. You'll get hypothermia, if you haven't got it already."

Then he looked at the hired hand and yelled, "Joe, take the rig and tell the doctor to go to William and Martha's, then take the rig home. I don't want you out in this storm more than you need to be. My home isn't far from here. I'll take Melinda home and get her warm. Make sure that Martha knows where she is, all right?"

Joseph nodded, whipped the reins, and down the road he sped. Gilbert tucked the shawl tightly around Melinda and then wrapped his arm around her, leading her to his house. The howling wind fought them all the way. They leaned into it to keep their balance and soon they reached his home. Tugging at the door, he finally pulled it open and pushed Melinda through as he pulled it shut.

Melinda stumbled, but Gilbert quickly grabbed hold of her to steady her. She was shivering uncontrollably and when she tried to thank him, she could not speak. The only words that came out were in the form of a stutter. Her mind was in a cloud and she could not think. When Gilbert asked her a question, she did not understand what he said and she felt confused.

Gilbert had seen hypothermia before and he recognized the signs. He knew that hypothermia was not only caused by freezing temperatures but also by improper clothing, wetness, and fatigue. Melinda had been struggling with the wind for quite some time, and her body was exhausted. And a thin dress with a couple of petticoats hardly consti- tuted proper clothing for a blizzard.

Quickly, Gilbert took her to the fireplace, which had a warm and comforting fire blazing within. He pulled the frozen and icy wrap off her shoulders and dropped it to the floor. He noticed her dress was caked with icy snow. He knew that as soon as it began to melt, she would be soaked to the skin if she weren't already.

Jenny walked into the living room and saw Melinda shaking. Gilbert looked at his daughter and said, "Jenny, I need your help. Quickly take Miss Gamble to my room and take off her frozen clothes and put my robe on her. Then bring her back here and we'll lay her on the sofa near the fire. I'll get some blankets to wrap around her."

Jenny did as she was told while Gilbert got several blankets and a pillow. When Jenny came back with Melinda, she said, "Pa, Miss Gamble isn't walking too good. I think that her legs are frozen."

"I wouldn't doubt it, Jenny."

Gilbert helped Melinda onto the sofa, tucked the robe around her freezing legs, and wrapped her in a blanket. He took another blanket and wrapped it around her head and neck. Then he grabbed a pillow and gently placed it under her head.

After Melinda had settled down comfortably on the sofa, Gilbert went into the kitchen and prepared some beef broth. One of the things he had learned was never to feed a hypothermia victim solid food or alcohol. Many times, people had the mistaken idea that they must feed the patient solid food so he can get his strength back, but that was a big mistake. And the idea that alcohol warms the victim up was the biggest mistake of all. In fact, Gilbert was well aware that alcohol did quite the opposite. Only warm liquids, such as broth, were appropriate.

Gilbert had learned a lot about hypothermia, simply because he lived in an area where most people needed that knowledge to survive. Survival in the West had a lot to do with the knowledge one gained and Gilbert was very much aware of it.

As he stood beside the stove making beef broth, he realized how worried he felt. The only other person he had ever worried about was his own daughter. It had seemed as if Jenny were his whole world, but for the first time in eight years, he found that he could open his heart up to another person. He found that he could even worry about someone other than his own daughter. This was a new feeling for him.

Gilbert looked at Jenny and gave her a loving smile. He loved her dearly and she knew it. When they rode side by side on their horses, she was his companion. But now, he wondered if he could have another companion as well. Jenny seemed to love Melinda and she had hinted at the fact that she wanted Melinda in the family. So, if he made the choice to marry her, Jenny would be happy, too. And that was very important to him. Jenny had to approve or he could not do it.

"Pa, shall I rub her arms and legs to warm them up?"

Gilbert shook his head. "No, dear. That would be the worst thing you can do. When someone has hypothermia, the first part that needs to get warm is the body. You could do her harm if you did that."

"All right, Pa. What should I do?"

"How about if you give her this broth that I made. It will warm up her insides."

Gilbert scooped the broth into a small bowl and then handed the bowl and spoon to Jenny. Gently, he pulled the covers away from Melinda's face so Jenny could feed her. Her face was still bright red and Gilbert moaned silently, extremely worried. As he watched Melinda, she seemed to shiver uncontrollably and his heart went out to her.

Jenny began to spoon-feed her as she talked to Melinda, but she did not respond. Jenny looked up at her father. "Pa, she's not listening. Is she all right?"

"Yes, she'll be all right. One of the signs of hypothermia is not being able to speak and comprehend what is going on. A person may be able to walk with hypothermia, yet not have their senses clear. But after she swallows enough broth, then she'll begin to warm up and her mind will become clear again. Just give her time, Jenny."

After Jenny fed her, Melinda slipped into a deep sleep. Her body was exhausted from fighting with the wind and from struggling to get warm. Gilbert went out to check on the animals and make sure the barn door was still shut. With a wind this powerful, the door could be blown open and even fly off its hinges. The last time they had a wind like this, it had taken someone's roof right off the barn.

Jenny stayed with Melinda and silently read a book. Every now and then, she would look up and check to see if Melinda was all right. When Melinda awoke and found herself with Jenny, she did not even remember how she had gotten there.

Jenny quickly put Melinda's mind at ease. "Oh, don't worry, Miss Gamble. My pa told me that when one gets hypothermia, your brain can't think and you don't know what's happening. That's why you didn't know how you got here. You have hypothermia. I was really worried about you. You kept shivering and wouldn't stop."

Melinda smiled at the maturity of Jenny's voice. "You certainly know a lot about hypothermia."

"Pa taught me. He knows everything."

Melinda smiled again. "I'm sure he does. But how about the doctor? Did he get to Uncle William on time?"

Gilbert had just opened the door as she spoke and he answered her question. "Yes. I sent Joe on ahead to get him."

"Joe? Who's he?"

"My hired hand. I sent him on ahead to get the doctor. When I noticed that you were shivering and began stuttering, I got real worried and brought you here immediately. I'm sure the doctor has taken care of William by now."

Melinda watched Gilbert as he took off his boots and placed them next to the door. Then he unbuttoned his coat and hung it on a hook by the door. He turned and smiled at her. Gilbert's smile set her mind at ease and she knew that there was nothing to worry about.

Chapter 18
HYPOTHERMIA

Melinda fell into a deep sleep once again. Hypothermia had completely worn out her body and she needed all the rest she could get. Gilbert had learned that some of the symptoms to watch for in mild hypothermia were the stumbles, mumbles, fumbles, and grumbles, along with uncontrollable shivering, so when he noticed these symptoms in Melinda, he knew exactly what to do.

As she slept, the blizzard continued its fierce howling. The snowflakes whirled to the earth, some of them as large as a quarter. The snowdrifts mounted in size and seemed to grow against every home and barn in the valley. Gilbert cleaned the kitchen while Jenny cleaned the living room. He had put a roast beef in the oven and the aroma filled the room.

"Pa, how long do you think the blizzard will last?"

"Don't know, darlin'. It's coming down pretty hard. It'll last all night, I'm sure. Sometimes blizzards will last a few days."

"How about Miss Gamble, Pa?"

"The snow's coming down too thick for anyone to go out in. I had to push my way to the barn to milk and feed the cows this morning. There's no way I'm going out in this storm again until we absolutely have to. The wind near blew me over, Jen."

"Could the wind pick up a person, Pa?"

"Don't know. All I know is that it can certainly make a person struggle as you walk in it."

After Jenny swept the floor and dusted the living room, she put a tablecloth on the table. Gilbert pulled the roast out of the oven and set it on the table.

Melinda began to stir and opened her eyes as the smell of the roast beef wafted towards her. As she stretched, she said, "O-o-oh, that smells good."

Gilbert smiled. "It sure does. Jenny, only set the table with two plates and one bowl. Melinda here can only have beef broth."

"What?" Melinda said in a disappointed tone. "But that's not fair."

Gilbert chuckled and then became serious as he explained. "You don't seem to understand how lucky you were today, Melinda. If I hadn't come upon you, I hate to think what would have happened. Only beef broth for you, dear lady." Then he thought for a moment and he smiled at her in a teasing manner. "And maybe a few little pieces of roast beef."

Melinda laughed softly. "I'd better get dressed. I've got to head home."

Gilbert slowly shook his head. "Not in this weather, you don't."

"What do you mean?"

"Melinda, look out that window. You'll have to sleep in our guest room tonight."

Melinda brushed a lose curl from her eyes, stood, and then wrapped herself in her blanket as she slowly waddled over to the window. She did not quite have the strength to walk yet, but she needed to have a look at the weather. "Goodness. It's really coming down, isn't it?"

As she watched the snow with amazement, it seemed like a winter wonderland outside. She looked over at Gilbert and asked, "Did you say guest room?"

"Yup, sure did. About six years ago I built this place for Jenny and me. We have folks who live back East and in Salt Lake City, so I made an extra room for visitors. While you were asleep, I made up the bed. If the storm subsides tomorrow, I'll take you home."

Gilbert noticed Melinda fumbling to keep the blanket around her shoulders and he smiled in amusement. "The guest room is over there." He waved a hand in the direction of the room. "You can go check it out if you like."

Melinda felt unsteady on her feet, but she wanted to see the room. When she entered, she noticed the bed had a pretty blue patchwork quilt on it and there was a washstand beside the bed with a white china bowl and matching pitcher upon it. She found her dress hanging in the wardrobe. She touched it to see if it was dry, but it was slightly damp. Her petticoats were hanging next to them, still damp, also. She had never had to worry about such freezing weather in Boston except for the 1888 blizzard that had shocked everyone. There was so much to learn out here in the West. She pulled the blanket up around her neck. Then she walked over to the window and pulled the blue-flowered drapes aside. As she stood there watching the snowflakes, she thought it was almost mesmerizing. How could something so beautiful be so dangerous?

There was a knock at the open door of the bedroom and Melinda turned and saw Jenny. "Yes, Jenny? Come on in."

Jenny walked in. "Supper's ready, Miss Gamble." She touched the wet dress that was hanging in the wardrobe. "It's still wet. Boy, did I struggle to get this thing off you. There were so many buttons and ties and everything else. And because it was wet, I couldn't seem to pull it off very easy. It was covered with ice and snow. Well, at least I didn't have to hang up that heavy dress and them petticoats. Pa did it for me."

Melinda felt uneasy that Gilbert had hung up her clothes, yet she knew there had been no other alternative.

Jenny slowly shook her head. "That's sure a lot of petticoats and underwear, Miss Gamble. Is that what women have to wear all the time?"

"I'm afraid so, sweetie."

"Well, when I grow up I'm not going to wear all that stuff."

Melinda smiled at Jenny's frankness and led her toward the dinner table.

"When I grow up, I want to wear pants just like Pa. None of them petticoats and stuff."

Gilbert had been listening to the small talk coming from the bedroom and he began to grin. With a deep chuckle, he said, "Oh, is that so? Well, we'll see how you feel about it after you grow up a bit."

"Pa, I'm never changin' my mind. Petticoats and all that underwear are for ladies and I'm no lady. I'm a rancher's daughter. Did you see all those clothes, Pa?" She shook her head vigorously. "No, not for me, Pa. Never."

Gilbert chuckled at his daughter's determined attitude, but Melinda merely blushed at the subject. She was not used to discussing women's clothing and undergarments in front of a man.

Gilbert was amused by his daughter's openness but when he saw Melinda blush, he realized they had embarrassed her. He quickly pulled out a chair for Jenny and then one for Melinda so they could sit at the dinner table. Melinda sat on one side of the table with Jenny on her left and Gilbert on her right. After everyone settled down, Gilbert said a prayer over the food.

As they sat, Melinda listened to the discussions that Gilbert and Jenny were having. He was teaching his daughter the tricks of cooking a roast so that it was tender and would fall apart with the touch of a fork.

"You see, Jenny, you cook it for about four hours at a low temperature and make sure to constantly pour water over it every half hour. And make sure you have a lid on it, too. That way, it will fall apart easily and remain moist."

"Yes, Pa."

"Do you remember when I said that I'm not going out in this weather again until I have to?"

"Yes, Pa, I do."

"Well, after we eat you can come out to the barn with me to feed and water the horses. We can't neglect them because of cold weather, you know."

"All right, Pa."

After Melinda sipped her broth, she asked, "May I have some of that roast beef? I'd like to see how tender it is."

Gilbert smiled and handed her the plate. After dishing a small portion for herself, Melinda stuck her fork into the beef and it fell apart. She put a forkful in her mouth and as she chewed, it seemed to melt in her mouth. It was so tender that it did not take long to chew. It was lightly seasoned with salt and a little pepper and the beef was not dry at all. It was indescribably delicious.

Gilbert anxiously watched her eat her first bite. "Well?"

Melinda looked up and her eyes brightened. "Mmmm. Delicious. The best I've ever tasted in my whole life. And I'm not exaggerating, either. There's sure a lot that a teacher can learn from a rancher."

Gilbert chuckled. Melinda sure had a way with words. He noticed a few strands of hair that had loosened and fallen appealingly about Melinda's face. Gilbert reached over and gently moved a curl that had fallen next to her eyes. The touch of his finger sent a tingle down her spine and a rosy glow appeared on her face, which made Gilbert grin. He had never seen anyone who blushed as easily as she did.

After supper, Melinda and Jenny did the dishes while Gilbert sat and read. "What do you do here after supper, Jenny?" Melinda asked.

"After I take care of my horse, then we sit and read. Sometimes Pa has me read to him. He says that when we read, we are in a world of our own, an imaginary world. He says that books help us learn and that's important. He says if I want to be smart like you, Miss Gamble, I need to read."

Melinda smiled and looked over at Gilbert reading comfortably in an overstuffed chair. After she washed the last dish and dried her hands, she walked over to him and saw that he was reading a book by Jules Verne, *In Search of the Castaways*.

"I've heard of this French author before," she said.

Gilbert looked up from his reading and smiled. "You have? Have you read his books before?"

"No, I haven't. But I've heard that he writes fiction, sort of nonsensical stuff."

Gilbert looked amused. "Oh? Is that what you heard or is that your own opinion of his books? That they're sort of nonsensical!" He noticed that she had definite opinions and was not afraid to admit them.

"Well, it's my own opinion, but I haven't read his works so I guess that I should at least read one of his books before I make a judgment. What is the book about?" Melinda sat down on the sofa and leaned back as she listened.

"This book was written in 1868. It's a story about a couple of children who set off to find their father who has disappeared after a shipwreck. Their search is based on a message found in a bottle, which was cast into the ocean by Captain Grant after the shipwreck. On their journey to find their father, they cross South America, Australia, and New Zealand. They encounter Indians in America, Bushrangers in Australia, and Maoris in New Zealand. On their journey, they are almost drowned in the floods of the Patagonian pampas, an avalanche sweeps them away, and a condor carries off the young boy. But, of course, he's saved. It wouldn't be right to get rid of one of the children, now, would it?" Gilbert grinned as he watched the interest in her eyes. "What I like most about Verne is that he describes the sights and sounds that the travelers see and hear. It helps me feel like I'm actually there."

When he saw how interested Melinda looked, he continued, "Melinda, let me share a paragraph with you so you can understand what I mean. Verne is describing what it looks like at the tops of the Andes Mountains." Gilbert flipped through a few pages and then read, "'The whole aspect of the region had now completely changed. Huge blocks of glittering ice, of a bluish tint on some of the declivities, stood up on all sides, reflecting the early light of morn.'"

"That's beautiful, Gilbert. I see what you mean."

Melinda saw a side of Gilbert that she had never seen before and she was impressed. This man, whom she had always referred to as a "rugged rancher," had another side to him. He loved to read and he could understand and enjoy the beautiful descriptions in a book.

While Gilbert and Jenny were feeding their horses in the barn, Melinda searched through the books on the bookshelf. There were plenty of books on farming and ranching, and on the care of children. He had more books by Jules Verne: *From the Earth to the Moon, Twenty Thousand Leagues under the Sea, A Journey to the Center of the Earth,* and *Around the World in Eighty Days.* He even had plenty of children's books. When he told Jenny that books were important, he clearly meant it. Melinda thumbed through the children's books and found *Black Beauty*. She pulled it out and searched through the pages. It looked new and the pages were stiff. She could tell the book had not been read yet.

Melinda sat down on the sofa and arranged her robe around her legs so she was comfortable and modest and then put the blanket on her lap. She listened to the fire crackle and the warmth of it filled the house while the blizzard was howling outside.

It was not long until Gilbert and Jenny opened the door. They were stomping their feet on the porch and laughing.

Jenny giggled, "Pa, next time we race to the house, I'm sure to win. Just you wait."

Melinda sat on the sofa watching with a smile. "Jenny, I found one of my favorite books. How would you like me to read it to you until bedtime?"

Jenny walked over to Melinda with curiosity. Looking at the book, she noticed a picture of a horse on the cover. Her face brightened with interested and with a lilt in her voice, she said, "All right. How about now?"

"First, let me tell you a little about the author of this book. Anna Sewell was born in 1820 and she wrote only one book at the age of 56. The sad thing is that it was published just before she died, in 1878. This book is about the life of a horse. In fact, it's from the viewpoint of a horse. Black Beauty is the narrator."

Upon hearing this, Jenny became excited. Melinda knew how much she loved horses. They seemed to be her life and she never neglected her own horse for anything. After riding Lilly, she would brush her down and feed and water her just as her father had taught her. Gilbert had taken special care to teach his daughter the responsibilities of caring for her own horse.

Jenny cuddled next to Melinda and leaned her head against her shoulder. Melinda opened the book and began to read, "'The first place that I can remember was a large pleasant meadow with a pond of clear water in it. Some shady trees leaned over it, and rushes and water lilies grew at the deep end...'"

Gilbert listened to the sweet tones of Melinda's voice as he washed up. After wiping his hands dry, he quietly walked over to his overstuffed chair and relaxed as he listened to *Black Beauty*. He had recently purchased it for his daughter, but they had not had the chance to read it yet. Gilbert watched his daughter's interest in the book and how sweetly she cuddled up to Melinda.

He noticed the inflections of Melinda's voice as she read and how she would make the story interesting with each emotion she conveyed. Gilbert's heart warmed towards Melinda as he realized how much he enjoyed being around her and how nice it was to have a woman in the house.

Time passed and when he looked at the clock and noticed it was 10:00, he ignored it. Both he and Jenny had gotten hooked on *Black Beauty* and he knew there would be no school tomorrow because of the weather. He felt there would be no harm in staying up late.

Melinda continued, "'We had a steep hill to go up. Then I began to understand what I had heard of. Of course I wanted to put my head forward and take the carriage up with a will, as we had been used to do. But no, I had to pull with my head up now, and that took all the spirit out of me, and the strain came on my back and legs...'"

164

Gilbert watched Melinda's eyes as she read and he noticed what a pleasant voice she had. He had never seen her in this setting before. For the first time, he saw the gentler side of her and he seemed to enjoy it very much.

Melinda continued, "'Day by day, hole by hole our bearing reins were shortened, and instead of looking forward with pleasure to having my harness put on as I used to do, I began to dread it.'"

As everyone listened, Melinda finished the last few sentences and then put a marker in the book. When she closed the book, she looked at Jenny. "It's time for bed. We'll finish tomorrow. What do you say?"

Jenny hopped up and gave Melinda a hug. Then she went to her father, kissed him on the cheek, and hugged him. "'Night, Pa." Looking over at Melinda, she said, "Now don't forget. After breakfast we read again."

Gilbert cut in, "Whoa, girl. You two can't finish this book without me. I'm hooked. I have chores to do in the morning. You have to wait for me. Promise to wait?"

Melinda and Jenny laughed softly at Gilbert wanting to be included in story time and agreed to wait, and then everyone headed for bed.

After the house had settled down and Melinda lay in bed, she heard Gilbert's soft deep voice through the walls, "All right, young lady. Don't forget your prayers. When you're done, I'll tuck you in."

"Hey, Pa. I'm too old to be tucked in. I'm eight years old."

"All right, if you say so. But you're never too old to be tickled."

Jenny began giggling uncontrollably.

"Stop, Pa, I surrender," she said between giggles. "You can tuck me in after all."

Melinda smiled. She had never seen this playful side of Gilbert before. In fact, this was the longest time they had been in the same room without an argument. She remembered how uneasy she had felt when they had stood together beneath the mistletoe at Christmastime, but now she did not feel uneasy. She felt different around Gilbert now; quite the opposite, in fact. It was a comfortable feeling, and she liked that feeling very much.

Chapter 19
THOMAS MOORE

The following morning, Gilbert was up bright and early, feeding and watering the cattle. After stomping his feet on the porch, he came inside, took off his boots, and hung his coat on the hook. Then he woke his daughter up to help him make breakfast.

Melinda heard the rattling of pans and quickly arose. She saw fresh water in the white china pitcher on the washstand with a wash rag and a towel next to it. Gilbert had quietly walked in while she was asleep and put fresh water in the pitcher for her so she could wash up. He had even placed a clean hairbrush on the small table for her. Quickly, she washed her face, neck, shoulders, arms, and hands. She felt refreshed once again and it felt so good.

When Melinda looked at the brush beside the bowl, she smiled at Gilbert's efforts to make her comfortable. She brushed her dark tresses and then placed her hair loosely upon her head and secured it with her combs. As she fixed her hair, she thought of yesterday and how she owed her life to Gilbert and Jenny. In fact, she owed her life to Gilbert twice now. Melinda had heard how dangerous hypothermia was. She could have been much worse if Gilbert had not found her in time. She had heard of people who had actually died from it.

After fixing her hair, Melinda slipped her dress over her pantalets and camisole and buttoned her dress up. Today, she would not wear her cumbersome petticoats. As she buttoned her dress, she began to giggle softly as she remembered what Jenny had said about all the buttons and petticoats. She was such a darling child and was not afraid to express her feelings.

When Melinda walked into the living room, she felt the warmth of the fireplace and heard the fire crackling gently. It felt so warm and cozy in this part of the house.

When she saw Gilbert cooking at the stove, she asked, "May I help you?"

Gilbert turned his head from the sizzling bacon and their eyes met. "Sure. Set the table. The plates are to the right of the sink. Thank you." He watched her as she took the plates from the cupboard. "Did you sleep well?"

Melinda glanced over at him. "Yes, I did. I slept very well and very warm. Thank you. And I would like to thank you for the brush and fresh water."

"It was nothing. I tried not to wake you up, but I knew you would need it this morning. After breakfast, Jenny and I have to check on the horses, brush them down, feed and water them. Then we can finish that story."

Melinda smiled. "It's a deal. While you two are out, I'll wash the dishes and clean up. How's the weather outside? Is it better?"

"Yes, a little. It's not coming down so hard today, but the wind is a devil to be out in. I'm hoping the wind will die down by tonight. I know you're anxious to get home. But we'll make you comfortable until it's safe to go home."

After breakfast, Melinda started the dishes and began humming a tune. She enjoyed singing as she did her chores. She looked around the room and she noticed that there were no pictures on the walls. This was a "man's home" with no feminine frills whatsoever. There was an oak gun cabinet, mounted deer antlers above the fireplace, and an old fifteen-inch bowie knife set upon hooks, hanging on the wall as a decoration. Everything about it was masculine.

While Jenny was brushing her horse in the comfort of the barn, she heard the wind howling. "Pa, I sure hate the wind."

"So do I, Jenny."

"When do you suppose it will stop?"

Gilbert shrugged his shoulders as he brushed his own horse. "Don't know. Maybe tonight or tomorrow morning."

"Pa."

"Yes, darlin'?"

"In a way, I don't want the wind to stop and in another way, I wish it would."

"Why is that, Jenny?"

"Well, Pa, if it stops, I won't have to hear all that howlin'. But then Miss Gamble will be leaving and I don't want her to leave. I like her, Pa. I like her a lot. So, if it doesn't stop, she'll have to stay."

Gilbert chuckled. "It does feel good to have her around, doesn't it? We haven't had a lady in the house before, have we?"

"Nope. We haven't."

After they finished, Jenny stepped out of the barn and looked at her father mischievously. "Run, Pa!"

And off she fled with Gilbert trailing after her.

When Jenny hit the porch first, she laughed. "Beat you this time."

Gilbert laughed and patted her back. "No fair, Jenny. You gave me no warning. I wasn't ready."

"Hey, Pa, haven't you always taught me to be ready at all times?"

"Oh, and that includes races?"

"Yup!"

Gilbert chuckled at her sense of humor. It reminded him of his own. As they stomped the snow off their feet, they walked into the house and stood in reverent awe at what they heard and saw.

Melinda had her sleeves rolled up, an apron tied around her slender waist, and she was cleaning the cabinets and table with a dishcloth while singing. Melinda's voice was rich, sultry, and mellow. Her tone was pure and expressive. Her voice, to be sure, was nothing short of angelic and Gilbert stood with his hat in hand, watching Melinda with admiration. Neither he nor Jenny moved a muscle as they listened.

Believe me if all those endearing young charms,
Which I gaze on so fondly today,

Were to change by tomorrow and fleet in my
*   arms*
Like fairy-gifts fading away.

The simple words were beautiful with a very special message. When Melinda looked up and saw them watching her, she smiled and continued singing.

Thou wouldst still be adored as this moment
*   thou art.*
Let thy loveliness fade as it will,
And around the dear ruin each wish of my
*   heart*
Would entwine itself verdantly still.

Gilbert and Jenny hung up their hats and coats and slipped their boots off in silence.

Melinda looked over at them and said, "That's one of my favorite songs. I'm part Irish. Thomas Moore was a great Irish poet. He was born in 1779 and died in 1852. He wrote the most romantic poetry I've ever read."

Gilbert washed up at the sink and then sat in his over-stuffed chair and watched her clean the table.

Melinda looked at Gilbert. "There's a story that is told about the song I just sang that touches me deeply." Melinda put the rag down and picked up a dishtowel and began wiping the dishes that had been washed. "The story is that Thomas Moore was away on business for quite some time. While he was gone, his wife was struck with smallpox. The illness had disfigured her face and she was so ashamed and embarrassed that she locked herself in her bedroom. When

Thomas Moore came home and found her locked in her room, he asked her to unlock the door." Melinda stopped what she was doing and looked at Gilbert and Jenny. "But she would not unlock it. She was ashamed of what she looked like. Moore told her that it didn't matter to him, but it did to her. She wanted to look pretty for the man she loved. When Moore realized that she wouldn't give in, he went to his desk and wrote a poem for his wife. The poem he wrote was what I just sang. When he slipped the poem under her door, she picked it up and read it. After reading about his undying love, her heart softened and she opened the door and let him in."

Melinda continued drying the dishes and putting them away. The room was silent and no one said a word. Gilbert watched Melinda work and he noticed how graceful she moved as she put each dish and plate in its place. The story had touched him and so did Melinda's presence.

Gilbert's love grew for this woman as she opened yet another mystery about herself. This woman had tenderness, something he had not seen before. After all, almost every encounter with her up to this point had been quite fiery. Yet she was exciting during those times, too. What determination! When she had an opinion, no one could thwart her. Yes, she was quite self-willed but he would never tell her so again, because Gilbert did not want to risk Melinda's wrath. He quickly found out how she hated that word, even if it were true. Gilbert smiled at the memory of that day. Yes, she was a fiery individual.

Gilbert's memory went back to two weeks ago when he had picked her up at the terminal. That was the first time he had held her in his arms. It had felt so good to hold her.

That encounter had stirred feelings within himself that he thought were dormant. She had responded to his touch and seemed to melt into his arms like a mold.

"That was it, a mold," he thought to himself. It was as if she fit there perfectly and was meant to be in his arms. As he thought of that day, his heart fluttered and he knew that he had fallen deeply in love with her.

Suddenly he awoke from his daydream as Melinda asked, "Are you ready to finish *Black Beauty*?"

She hung the wet dishtowel up to dry and then wiped her hands on her apron. After removing the apron, she hung it on the hook where she had found it. Then she walked over to the sofa, picked up the book, and turned to the spot she had marked.

Jenny cuddled up to Melinda on the sofa and put her head against her shoulder as Melinda read. After a while, Melinda heard a few sniffles from Jenny as she read, "'My life was now so utterly wretched that I wished I might, like Ginger, drop down dead at my work and be out of my misery.'"

Melinda took the edge of her skirt and wiped Jenny's tears away and then hugged her. "Shall we stop and have lunch?"

Jenny shook her head. "I've just got to see how this turns out, Miss Gamble."

"But, Jenny, my voice is tired. I must rest. Aren't you hungry?"

At this announcement, Gilbert hopped up and began to fix something for lunch. When Melinda saw what he was doing, she walked toward him, "May I help?"

"Sure. You can cut the bread while I cut the roast beef from yesterday. We can have roast beef sandwiches."

"Sounds good to me." Melinda smiled and began cutting the bread. "Did you make this bread?"

"Sure did." He turned to face her and said softly, "Melinda, I just want you to know that it sure has been good to have you around."

"It has?"

"Yes, it has." Then he turned to her and grinned. "And don't ask me why. I'm not going through that again."

Melinda laughed softly, remembering what had happened at the train station.

"You know, Melinda, we have broken a record."

"What record is that?"

"We have been together now for two days without one argument."

Melinda burst into laughter. "Now that's a miracle, isn't it?"

She buttered the bread and added relish, salt, and pepper. Then Gilbert placed several thin slices of beef on it.

After Gilbert wiped his hands clean, he looked into her eyes. "It's nice to work as a team rather than against one another, don't you think?"

Melinda smiled and nodded.

"So, you're Irish, eh?"

"Yes. My grandfather came over from Enniskean, Cork County, Ireland."

Gilbert grinned. "I've heard about the Irish tempers. I used to think it was a fable."

Melinda looked at him curiously and wondered if he was serious or teasing her. When she could not quite tell, she put her hands on her hips in a stubborn stance and stared into his eyes, saying in mock exasperation, "It *is* a fable. And you're not so innocent yourself, Mr. Roberts. I remember a time when you were quite upset at me and it had something to do with your cows getting loose."

She was teasing him and he knew it. This was the first time she had ever teased him and he liked her spirit.

Gilbert grinned and put both hands up in the air in surrender. "You're right and I shouldn't have said that. I remember I bit your head off that day. I'm sorry." Looking at his daughter, he said, "Jenny, get washed up. Lunch is ready."

Jenny grinned at the confrontation that she had just witnessed between her father and Melinda and then took off.

Melinda stood with her hands still on her hips as she watched Gilbert put the food on the table. She was having fun with him and was trying very hard to suppress a smile.

After Jenny left the room, Gilbert turned from the table and saw Melinda's stubborn stance, which was quite amusing. His eyes swept over her figure with interest. After a quick glance to see if Jenny was gone, he grinned and took large strides toward Melinda and stood in front of her. He slid his hands around her slender waist and embraced her tenderly.

"Why do I infuriate you so?" he whispered in her ear.

Melinda slightly gasped at his touch, and the warmth of his breath against her ear sent a shiver down her spine. She was not expecting this from Gilbert.

"You don't infuriate me, Gilbert. I…I don't know why I get upset over such little things."

Gilbert wrapped his arms around her and squeezed her gently, holding his hands firmly against her back. It did not take much before she melted into his arms and leaned her head against his shoulder.

As she sighed, Gilbert grinned. "Yup, it happened again. I just had to check to see if it was my imagination." Then he pressed his lips to her temple and gave her a lingering kiss.

Feeling the warmth of his lips against her face, she tried to keep her senses about her, but without much success. Finally, Melinda breathlessly asked, "What do you mean?"

Gilbert nuzzled his cheek next to hers and whispered, "I mean, when I hold you close to me like this, you seem to melt and mold into my arms like it's so natural. You're so soft and it feels so good to hold you, Melinda."

Melinda's heart began to swell at the tender words that Gilbert had just told her and she seemed to relax in his arms. She looked up into his eyes and wrapped her arms around his chest and held him tightly.

Aware of Melinda's embrace, Gilbert realized that she was experiencing the same feelings he was toward her, and he didn't want to release her. He looked down at the woman in his arms staring back at him and saw the fullness of her lips and a desire to kiss her rose within him. He leaned down toward her and was about to press his lips to hers when he heard a sound at the hallway.

Just then Jenny entered the room. Melinda's face flushed as she instantly pulled her hands up against Gilbert's chest and firmly pushed herself out of his arms. Then she wiped her hands on her skirt nervously. Gilbert grinned as he watched Melinda's face redden. Her blush was so amusing that he had to suppress a chuckle. He turned around and saw Jenny smiling at him.

"Sit down, Jenny. Let's eat."

As they sat at the table, Melinda was quiet. Her heart was still pounding rapidly and she tried to think of something to say. Looking up at Gilbert, she was still flushed and embarrassed. Then she said, "Uhm...how's the weather? May I go home today?"

Gilbert grinned at her beautiful rosy face. He seemed to enjoy embarrassing her. He tried to hold back a chuckle as he answered Melinda's question. "It's much better. You might be able to leave this afternoon."

Jenny spoke up. "No. I don't want you to leave. Please stay, Miss Gamble."

Melinda smiled as the original color came back to her cheeks. "I must, sweetie."

Gilbert quickly added, "Not until we finish *Black Beauty*, all right? What do you say?"

Melinda's heart filled with warmth as she saw his tender eyes watching her, full of hope. Then she nodded in agreement.

After lunch, Jenny and Melinda did the dishes while Gilbert read in his favorite chair. Gilbert had volunteered to help Melinda with the dishes, but she refused his help for two reasons. First, he had been cooking and waiting on her since she arrived. Second, Melinda felt she needed to protect her heart, especially after the way it had reacted when he embraced her. She knew she was falling in love with Gilbert, but she did not know how he truly felt about her. Melinda felt vulnerable and she needed to protect her heart until Gilbert was ready for a commitment. She realized that

Gilbert had concerns because he had voiced them on the way home from the terminal. She just had to wait until he was ready.

After the dishes were done, Melinda sat beside Jenny and finished the book. "'And here my story ends. My troubles are all over, and I am at home; and often before I am quite awake, I fancy I am still in the orchard at Birtwick, standing with my old friends under the apple trees.'"

Melinda closed the book and hugged Jenny. "I should go home now, Jenny."

Melinda realized that she needed to go home as soon as possible. Her love for this man was growing and until he was ready, she needed to get her life back into order again.

Upon hearing this, Gilbert immediately stood. "I'll get the buckboard ready. Joe brought it by this morning when he helped me milk and feed the cows."

It was late afternoon, the sun was beginning to set, and the ride home was chilly. The wind had calmed down and the cloudless sky left a crispness in the air. The ice on the bare branches of nearby trees and shrubs was sparkling with the evening sun. A rabbit scurried across the field, heading for shelter. They passed drifts and large mounds of snow as the horse trotted along the road.

Melinda was quiet as Gilbert looked toward her. Her cheeks were pink from the chill and she looked absolutely lovely. He smiled at her as he reined in the horse. "You're home, Melinda."

Gilbert hopped down from the buckboard and then offered to help her down. The step along the side of the buckboard was icy, so she held onto the back of the seat as Gilbert held out his hand. Her foot slipped on the icy step and she grabbed tightly onto the back of the seat to steady herself.

"Wait. Let me help you down," Gilbert said softly.

He held both hands out while she stood beside the seat. She leaned toward him and put her hands on his shoulders while he slipped his hands around her waist and lifted her down slowly. Gilbert's physical strength was obvious as he slowly lifted her down until her feet touched the ground.

As Melinda stood with her back against the buckboard, she was aware of his hands still around her waist. She was also conscious of his closeness as she felt the warmth of his breath against her face. Gilbert stood beside her and gazed into her eyes with tenderness. Melinda's heart beat furiously from the touch of his hands around her as he lingered for a moment. He seemed to be studying the contours of her face and as his eyes wandered to her mouth, she could tell that he wanted to give her a kiss—the kiss of which he had been cheated when Jenny had interrupted them. But for some reason, he chose not to. His magnetic charm tugged at her heart and she could not deny that she was in love.

"I'll walk you to the door so you don't slip."

"Thank you, Gilbert."

Then he dropped his hands from her waist, stepped back, and took her arm to steady her. "I'm so glad you don't call me Mr. Roberts anymore. It sounded so formal."

Melinda laughed softly at his comment as she opened the door of her home. She turned to face him, but he was already heading back to the buckboard before she could thank him. She watched him leave, but he did not turn and look back. To Melinda, it was a sign of affection when someone turned and gave one last glance or smile. Why didn't he turn and take one last look at her?

She knew that something was bothering him and that he still was not ready for a commitment or he would have taken the opportunity to tell her his true feelings when he had her cornered at the buckboard. His eyes had been so fixed upon her as he held her at the buckboard and Melinda knew that he wanted to say something, but didn't.

Inside, she wished that he would have taken her in his arms and held her and given her the same lingering kiss that he had given her at the terminal. Melinda's chest became heavy and a few tears stung her eyes. The pain in her breast intensified and her heart felt as if it would break. Why did she have to fall in love with a man who was afraid of commitment?

Chapter 20
VALENTINE'S DAY

Three weeks passed and Gilbert had not seen Melinda at all except in passing at church or in town. He had been purposefully avoiding her because he had concerns that he had to work out before he could court her. Valentine's Day was coming in less than a week. The community was going to have a Sweetheart's Dance and Gilbert wondered whether or not he should go. Would Melinda be there? As he fixed supper alongside Jenny, he saw her look curiously at him.

"Pa, are you going to the dance?"

"Don't know, Jenny."

"I know you like Miss Gamble, Pa. No need tryin' to hide it from me."

Gilbert laughed. "How do you know?"

"It's in your eyes, Pa. You can't hide it. I saw the way you looked at her and watched her move about when she didn't know you were watching."

"You're too smart for your breeches."

"Are you goin' to give her a valentine?"

"A valentine?"

"Yes, Pa. You always give a valentine to a sweetheart."

"But, Jenny, she's not my sweetheart."

"You could've fooled me when I saw you two in the kitchen. You were holdin' her, Pa. And she blushed. No lady ever blushes unless she likes a man. She's your sweetheart and you don't even know it." Jenny giggled when she saw her father shake his head as if denying the fact. "Pa, send her a poem. She'll like it."

"A poem? Why?"

"Because it's romantic. Don't you know anything about romance, Pa? Let me tell you the story about Valentine's Day. Miss Gamble taught us about Saint Valentine at school. You see, Saint Valentine was a priest in Rome. A bad ruler named Claudius wanted to have a large army but the men wouldn't join because they didn't want to leave their wives. So Claudius outlawed marriage so the men would join the army. But Valentine still married couples in secret. Finally, he was caught and thrown in jail."

Gilbert began setting the table with a couple of plates, cups, and forks as he listened. "So is that how Valentine's Day got started? Because he continued to marry couples?"

"Not exactly, Pa. He fell in love when he was in prison. The daughter of the prison guard visited him. They would sit and talk for hours and they fell in love. The day he was going to be executed, Valentine left a note for her, thanking this woman for her friendship and love. Then he signed it, 'Love, from your Valentine.'" Jenny walked to the kitchen chair and picked up her notebook with her notes from school and read, "He wrote that note on the day they put him to death on A.D. February 14th, 269." She looked up from her notes and said, "He was a hero and a romantic person, Pa. So, that's why we have Valentine's Day. Understand?"

Her grown-up attitude and intelligence impressed Gilbert quite a bit. As Jenny turned around to place her book on the chair, Gilbert grabbed his daughter around the waist and playfully tickled her. As she burst into laughter, he asked, "How did you remember so much about this St. Valentine? You're such a smart little girl."

Jenny enjoyed her father's playful ways, but it did not take long until she squirmed out of her father's arms and bolted into the living room.

Gilbert grinned. "Well? Answer my question."

As Jenny settled down, she took a deep breath and answered, "I listen, Pa. Besides, Miss Gamble makes us take notes. Sometimes she writes it on the board and we can copy it."

"I see." Gilbert nodded as he placed a plate of sandwiches on the table. "So, what kind of poem should I give Miss Gamble?" Then with a mischievous glint in his eyes, Gilbert grinned from ear to ear and said, "I know, how about the poem called 'My Fancy' by Lewis Carroll? I've read it to you so many times that I have it memorized. That's a real romantic one, don't you think?"

Jenny giggled. She remembered it very well. He had read it to her many times and it always made her laugh.

Then Gilbert continued, "It tells all the things that you love about your sweetheart." He stood at attention and then quoted,

She has the bear's ethereal grace,
The bland hyena's laugh,
The footstep of the elephant,
The neck of the giraffe.
I love her still, believe me,
Though my heart its passion hides;
She is all my fancy painted her,
But, oh, how much besides.

Jenny laughed so hard that her sides began to ache. After a while she put her hands on her hips in mock exasperation. "Now, Pa, if you don't become serious about this, you'll lose her for sure. I've noticed the superintendent has been making eyes at Miss Gamble lately. His name is Henry and when he talks to her, she smiles back at him. Sometimes he makes her laugh."

Gilbert became sober and stood a while in thought, rubbing his chin. "Hmmm, Henry's been paying attention to her?"

"Yup."

"How much attention?"

"Quite a lot, Pa."

"A lot?"

"Yup. Are you goin' to write her a poem now? He even made her some fake flowers and gave 'em to her to put on her desk at school and he put perfume all over 'em. They sure stink up the classroom. After he gave 'em to her, Miss Gamble smiled and said thank you all sweet like. You had better give her a nice poem, Pa. And I mean it."

Gilbert gave her a subdued half smile. "All right. I'll think about it. Right now it's time to eat and I believe it's your turn to say the blessing on the food."

During the rest of the week, Gilbert heard gossip in town all about Henry and Melinda. He heard about how Henry was bragging that they had been dating since December, which annoyed him to no end. Gilbert started to get worried and nervous about it. Then he noticed that he was becoming edgy and ornery with everyday chores. One time he actually kicked the bucket he was milking into. It flew across the barn and hit the wall at great speed, splattering the milk everywhere. When Joseph asked him how his bucket ended up against the wall, he just said, "My foot slipped."

Why did he feel so jealous about Henry? Melinda was a beautiful woman and it was only natural that others would be interested in her. She had a right to date whomever she pleased. After much examination of his emotions, Gilbert knew that if there had been any doubt of his being in love with her before, there certainly wasn't now.

Gilbert remembered the first time he had seen her wading in the stream and how she had laughed so delightfully as she watched a couple of birds flying above her. She had exuded such purity and innocence as she waded barefoot down the creek. Gilbert chuckled as he remembered that day. He remembered how flustered he had been when he saw this graceful and beautiful woman heading his way, holding her skirts above the water.

Then he remembered her stormy eyes as they flamed with anger when he had tried her patience. Gilbert grinned at the memory of it. He thought about Melinda's timid and uneasy face he had gazed upon as they stood beneath the mistletoe. He noticed that she felt insecure with him so near and when he took her hand, he could see the relief in her face.

The memory of her gentle and warm kiss at the terminal remained etched in his mind, as well as the memory of her voice singing as she cleaned the cabinets of his home and her gentleness as she read *Black Beauty*.

Gilbert remembered how she had blushed when Jenny caught him hugging her in the kitchen just as he was about to give her a kiss, and he remembered how her blush had affected him, also.

Gilbert knew that he had to do something if he didn't want to lose her. He had to write a poem and he had to go to the dance. He also needed to have a long talk with her about something he had held inside for years.

Gilbert never cared for dances because he had never learned how to dance. But if Melinda was going to be there, he had to be there too. He could socialize and that wouldn't be so bad. He had a few friends who went to the dances every month. He could visit with them until he had a chance to take Melinda aside. His plan was to talk to Melinda and let her know his concerns and see what she had to say. He had never expressed all his concerns to anyone before. He had been too embarrassed. This would be his first time. How would she react to it?

Gilbert sat at the table with a pencil in hand and a paper before him. After giving it much thought, he knew what to write. The first encounter they had had was so delightful that he decided to put it into poetry. After an hour of writing, erasing, rewriting, and suffering through a bundle of nerves, he finally finished his rough draft. Then he very neatly wrote his poem on a fresh piece of paper, put it in an envelope, and sealed it.

Looking at the envelope, Gilbert breathed a deep sigh, wondering how Melinda would respond to such an unprofessional poem as his. He wrote her name on the envelope and stuck it in his pocket. Immediately he saddled his horse and rode out to Martha's home. He hoped to surprise her by leaving the poem where Melinda could find it before she arrived from school. His heart was beating erratically from nervousness as he knocked on the door. When Uncle William answered, Gilbert asked for Martha. For some reason, he felt it would be easier to give the envelope to her.

As he stood in the living room waiting for Martha, he noticed a large box of chocolate candies on the coffee table with Melinda's name on it. Gilbert inched his way over to them and peered down at the box, which read, "Happy Valentine's Day, from Henry."

A twinge of jealousy and embarrassment shot through him. Gilbert was giving Melinda a silly poem while Henry had given her a large box of candy. She would surely love the candy so much more. Feeling embarrassed, he was about to slip the envelope back into his pocket and leave just as Martha entered the room.

Before he had time to hide the envelope, Martha spoke. "Is that for Melinda?"

She pointed to the envelope in his hand and he looked down at it. Melinda's name was written upon it in plain sight. There was nothing he could do about it now. He nodded and gave it to her reluctantly.

Feeling embarrassed and awkward, Gilbert didn't know what to say, so he turned around to leave.

Martha touched his arm and said with kindness, "She really likes you, Gilbert. She likes you a lot."

Surprised, he turned around and asked. "Do you really think so?"

"I know so. It's in her eyes. Whenever I bring your name up at the table, her eyes will sparkle and she'll listen tentatively. When I bring up Henry's name, she doesn't seem to care. And this week when we saw you riding your horse in town and you waved to us as you passed, I looked into her eyes and they were glowing. Gilbert, she's in love. I can tell."

Gilbert gave a broad smile.

"Gilbert, what are you waiting for? Are you not sure of your heart?"

"Martha, we are so different. That's what bothers me. She may not be able to handle the West. It's tough here and she may not be happy after a while. An Eastern lady and a rancher is not a great combination."

"Do you love her, Gilbert?"

He looked into her eyes and saw tenderness and understanding. He hesitated and then answered, "Yes, I do."

"Gilbert, I came from the East and I love it here."

"But everyone isn't like you, Martha. You're a tough woman and the West didn't scare you."

"Gilbert," Martha said softly with concern lacing her eyes. "I know that something is bothering you and I don't know what it is. But I have a feeling that it's much more than just your differences. What are you afraid of, Gilbert? Why are you worrying so much about Melinda becoming unhappy here in the West or even being tough enough?"

Without thinking, Gilbert blurted out, "I'm not making the same mistake twice."

Then he abruptly turned and walked out the door without further explanation.

Chapter 21
THE POEM

When Melinda arrived home from school, she immediately saw the gifts on the coffee table. She noticed the box of candy was from Henry and then she saw the envelope that read, "To Melinda, from Gilbert." Her spirits soared and her heart fluttered with joy as she quickly ran upstairs to open her letter.

After placing her books on a small table in her room, she sat upon her bed, crossed her legs, and opened the envelope with care. Sliding the paper out excitedly, she unfolded it and read,

When first I came upon you
Wading in the stream,
You held your skirts with one hand.
You were barefoot and free.

Your cheeks were rosy from the sun,

An auburn curl upon your cheek,
Your eyes were green like shamrocks,
And your laughter delighted me.

Who is this creature, I asked myself?
A nymph, a charming lady.
Who is this beautiful person
That brings happiness to me?

Tears of joy filled her eyes as she pressed the poem to her breast. The poem was beautiful and she was impressed that he remembered each little thing about her on that first day they met, just as she remembered him. She remembered his soft, deep voice and the flushed look of embarrassment when he had caught himself staring at her.

As she prepared for the dance that evening, she wondered if Gilbert would be at the dance so she could thank him for the poem. Henry had asked her if he could escort her to the dance and she had accepted. Anxious to get ready, she hurried downstairs to get something to eat.

When she entered the kitchen, Aunt Martha looked at her and asked nonchalantly. "Did you see the gifts on the coffee table?"

"Yes, I did," she said in a coy manner.

"Wasn't that sweet of Henry?"

"It certainly was."

"I noticed that Gilbert dropped something by, also."

When she saw Martha searching her eyes curiously, Melinda nodded with a smile. The happiness she felt was indescribable and she could not put it into words.

As she helped her aunt fix the meal, Martha looked at her and said, "I finished your dress today. It's going to look lovely on you, Melinda."

"Do you think so?"

"I know so. I hung it up in your wardrobe. After we eat, go try it on."

Melinda immediately wrapped her arms around her aunt and gave her a lingering hug. "Thank you, Aunt Martha. I truly appreciate it."

When Henry picked Melinda up for the dance, she was not quite ready. He waited impatiently and paced the living room floor. It took Melinda a little longer than usual to get ready and they were about half an hour late to the dance. As they entered the Social Hall, the music was already playing. Henry took her coat and left the room to hang it up while she stood alone at the entrance waiting for him.

Melinda looked like a valentine, dressed in a red silk gown that gathered at the waist and hung gracefully around her hips, skimming the tops of her shoes. The bodice of the dress was snugly fitted, which emphasized her slim waist and the gentle curves of her body. The neck was round with a wide collar that met at the shoulders and had white lace trimmed around the edges. The sleeves were gathered at the shoulder and hung freely to her elbows. There was nothing elaborate about the dress, but it did look elegant and the color seemed to compliment her creamy complexion. Her hair was in a loose bun with many small red and white silk flowers pinned in her rich auburn hair.

When Gilbert saw this vision of loveliness standing at the door, his mouth dropped open and his eyes widened with wonder. Her beauty had taken his breath away and he could not take his eyes off her. She looked absolutely radiant in red and her dress was very flattering to her figure. His eyes swept over her, taking in her beauty, and he felt speechless. When their eyes met, she smiled and his spirits rose and happiness overtook him.

"How can I possibly talk to her when she looks like this?" he thought to himself. "She's so...so..." He couldn't seem to find adequate words to express how he felt.

He watched Henry walk up to her, slide his hand around her waist, and lead her to the dance floor. Gilbert's eyes followed her and he noticed how gracefully she moved across the floor. She had such poise. She seemed as if she were as light as a feather with every movement she made. Her charm and gracefulness gave her a sort of ethereal beauty. It was a delight to watch someone with such ease in every step.

Gilbert's pleasant thoughts were suddenly interrupted. One of his friends walked up to him, pounded him on the back, and asked, "Gilbert, what are you doing here? I've never seen you at a dance function all the years I've known you."

"Just decided to try coming once. But this may be the first and last time you ever see me at one of these. I'm not a dancer."

"So, did you come for the food and to socialize?"

Gilbert grinned inside. He knew what he had come for but he was not about to tell them.

"Yup."

That was all he said. Soon the conversation went to farming, cattle, fencing, and all the rest of the gossip around town.

"Gilbert, I heard that new schoolteacher is dating Henry. They've been dating for some time now. I overheard Henry saying that he was going to ask her to marry him sometime soon. But I don't know when."

This was not what Gilbert wanted to hear. After noticing that Henry had danced with Melinda for six dances in a row, he wondered if Henry was going to monopolize her the whole evening. All he had to do was wait for the proper moment so he could get her alone.

When he saw Henry take her to the snack table to get a drink, Gilbert became quite annoyed with him. Frustrated, he wondered if he would ever get a chance to talk with her alone that evening. Then he noticed Henry's friends talking to him at the snack table and he turned his back on Melinda.

Gilbert knew this would be his only chance. He quickly strode across the Social Hall and grabbed Melinda's hand, pulling her toward the entrance and, once outside, shutting the door behind them.

"Melinda, if I have to kidnap you from Henry, then that's what I'll have to do."

Melinda laughed softly and smiled. "I'm glad because I've been wanting to talk to you, too. I wanted to thank you for that lovely poem." She hesitated for a moment, looking down at her shoes, and then continued in a softer tone, "It really touched my heart. No one's ever written a poem for me before. The thought that you actually wrote a poem just for me...oh, Gilbert..." The words would not come and emotion constricted her speech. She didn't know how to express enough gratitude.

Melinda looked up into Gilbert's eyes and he was touched. He could see how she felt as she spoke and he was pleased. "Melinda, let's walk and talk. If you get cold, we'll come back."

Gilbert took his coat off and wrapped it around her shoulders, then took her warm hand in his as they walked slowly in the snow. The touch of her hand was thrilling as they walked side by side. Gilbert wanted to talk, but the words would not come. He knew he needed to tell her of his concerns and see how she would react to them. But more than anything, he just wanted to be near Melinda and feel her sweet spirit.

The snow crunched beneath their feet with each step they took. The air was cool, but not crisp enough to freeze their ears and noses. Gilbert looked over at Melinda and gently squeezed her hand to let her know that he was glad to be with her.

When he squeezed her hand, Melinda's heart skipped a beat and she took a deep breath as she smiled back at him. She noticed that he looked quite dapper as they walked hand in hand. She had never seen him dressed like this before, in his black woolen vest and black bolo tie over a long-sleeved white shirt.

"Gilbert, how did you remember so much about me on that first day we met? You have such a good memory."

"Oh, my mind is like a steel trap...old and rusty."

Melinda began to laugh and Gilbert joined her.

"Gilbert, where are you originally from?"

"The outskirts of Salt Lake City."

"Is that where you met your wife?"

Melinda had broken the barrier between them without even knowing it. This was exactly what he needed to talk about and he needed to see her reaction. Now he could express his concerns.

"Yes. She and her parents had just arrived from the East. They had been here for six months when they decided they didn't like it in the West. They missed the East and all its social life. I had only known Molly for two months and I fell for her. We didn't know one another very well, but I didn't want her to leave, so I asked her to marry me. She accepted and we got married and moved here the day after we were married. Molly and I were very different and our goals were different, but I thought that our differences would mesh together into one and soon we would have very few differences. But it didn't work out that way and she was very unhappy."

"How were you different?"

Gilbert kicked a chunk of snow out of the way and looked at Melinda. "She was a city girl from the East. She loved parties and dances and the social life. I didn't. I was a farm boy and I wanted to have a ranch of my own. I loved her a lot, Melinda. I would have done anything for her. Everyone thought we had an ideal marriage because we never argued. She always wanted to please me, but that wasn't what I wanted. I wanted to know her opinions, her likes, and her dislikes. If we could only have had a few disagreements so I could've just known where I stood in our marriage, I would have liked it. I wanted to know her feelings inside but she kept them from me. I suspected she was unhappy and missed the East and all its finery. One day I found a letter she wrote to her parents that was lying on the table. She had expressed her unhappiness to them and her longing to return to the East for a visit. My heart wrenched when I read those words. Why hadn't she expressed them to me? Why couldn't we talk?"

Gilbert's voice became constricted with emotion and he quickly cleared his throat and continued. "When she was with child, her health went downhill because of the morning sickness. She couldn't seem to keep anything down. When I saw how unhappy she was, that was when I realized that the West was too tough for her, Melinda. And when Jenny was born, she died. I blamed myself for her death because I felt I should have been more in tune to her feelings and I wasn't. If I had only known how unhappy she was, then I would have tried even harder to make her life easier. We had only been married for nine months and then she was gone."

"But you can't blame yourself, Gilbert. Complications happen in pregnancy even in the city. And you say that because of your differences she was unhappy. That may not have been the reason. It may have been her pregnancy and not your differences at all, Gilbert. She had morning sickness and was miserable for several months. When one is miserable, that's when we long for those days that bring us the most joy and perhaps those happy memories are somewhere else, perhaps in our past. She was very happy in the East, so her longing to be with her parents was only natural. You have assumed that it was your differences, but you may have been wrong. Sometimes differences are good and we can help one another grow. My parents were as different as night and day. My father was a city lawyer. My mother was a country girl from Utah. She was a spiritual woman and my father knew nothing of spiritual things. But because of his love for her, he tried hard by reading the scriptures and going to church with her. When they married, their differences gradually decreased with time. But there were two differences that never changed—their personalities and temperaments."

"Temperaments?"

"Yes. My father is a calm and even-tempered man and my mother is vivacious and has the Irish temper..." she hesitated and looked up at Gilbert.

Gilbert grinned from ear to ear as he recalled what she had said earlier about an "Irish temper."

Melinda flushed a rosy color and then continued. "What I mean is that she has a mind of her own. No one can sway her decisions, unless she realizes she's wrong. She is a strong-headed woman, but my father loves her the way she is. So, you see, differences aren't always bad. They can complement a marriage. Besides, I know your wife must have loved you dearly and she knew that you wanted to be a rancher so she didn't complain. She wanted you to be happy. She must have had a great deal of love for you, Gilbert. And I can see why. You're a very gentle and loving man. You seem to care for others, including those who work for you."

Out of the door came Henry, yelling at the top of his voice, "Melinda. Hey, Melinda. Come on in. Let's dance." He sounded a little irritable and impatient.

"I'll be right there, Henry." She turned to Gilbert and gave a dry smile. "He brought me here. I must go, Gilbert."

Gilbert squeezed her hand gently to thank her for the words that she had said, but did not say a thing. He felt speechless after everything she had just told him.

Melinda felt the warmth of Gilbert's hand around hers as he squeezed it and then she reluctantly slid her hand from his. She slipped off his coat and handed it to him and then walked toward Henry. After a few steps, she stopped and turned around. Her love for this man was evident as she gave him one last glance. When their eyes met, she smiled lovingly and her eyes sparkled as she softly gazed into the depths of his dark eyes. Then she quickly turned and continued on her way.

As Gilbert watched her, he thought about what she had said to him. She had said that some differences could be valuable and help people grow while other differences diminish with time. As he thought about it, his wife's goals would become his goals and his goals would become hers. Gilbert liked that idea. Then he thought about the last thing she had said just before she left: "She must have had a great deal of love for you, and I can see why." He smiled. Melinda knew just how to uplift him and make him feel good about himself.

As he watched the woman in red approach the steps of the Social Hall, he saw her look up at Henry. They were discussing something and Henry was not happy at all. Melinda shook her head at him and then she put her hands on her hips in a stubborn and indignant stance.

Gilbert chuckled. He had seen that stance before and he knew that she was not happy. Then Henry tried to make up to her and put his arm around her shoulder, but Melinda pushed him away and stomped up the steps.

Gilbert chuckled again as he gazed after her. "What a spunky woman!"

Chapter 22
SKUNK OIL

In March, the weather warmed up and the snow was still in the tops of the mountains but was melting in the valley of Paris. The warmth created restlessness among the students and Melinda noticed that it was harder for them to concentrate on their studies.

During the week, Billy had caught a spider, tied a string tightly around its body, and then tied the string to a stick. He brought it to school and hid it in his desk. When the class was silently reading, he pulled it out and hung the stick over Peggy's head, dangling the spider in front of her face. When Peggy saw something wiggling in front of her, she lifted her eyes from her book and let out the most shrill and hideous scream one could ever imagine.

Billy quickly hid his stick in his desk, hoping Peggy would think the spider had come down from the ceiling. He could not help the euphoria he felt when she screamed and he instantly put his hand over his mouth to conceal his laughter, then looked at his book as if he were innocently reading. Melinda, however, had witnessed the whole thing.

Melinda told Billy that he could help her sweep the floor of the classroom and wash the blackboard for her after school was over. He accepted his duties without any argument.

Later, Melinda peacefully stood at the doorway of the school, enjoying the fresh air as the children played during recess. She had not seen Gilbert since the Valentine's Dance, but since their conversation that night she had realized what had been bothering him. He had blamed himself for his wife's death and felt that his wife could not handle the West. Melinda adored him and hoped she would be able to help him through his frustrations. She knew that their differences were causing him much concern.

As she leaned against the doorframe, she listened to the prattle of the children. Mark was only a few feet from her. He was a slim young man with sky-blue eyes, auburn hair, and freckles that covered his face. He was always cheerful and had a smile for anyone passing. Mark was telling Billy about the problem he had with skunks getting into his chicken coop and eating the eggs.

"So, do you know what Pa did, Billy? He went out in the dark with his rifle and just sat by the chicken coop waiting. Pretty soon the skunk showed up and Pa shot him. Boy, the smell from that skunk was disgusting."

"How big was he, Mark?"

"About as big as a cat with the purtiest white stripe right down its back. So, do you want to know what I did?"

"What?"

"When Pa told me to bury him in the morning, I drained the skunk oil from his glands first and put it in a little bottle."

"You did? I'd sure like to see it, Mark."

"Really? Come with me to my desk and I'll show you."

Mark and Billy walked past Melinda just as a fight broke out in the yard. Melinda ran to see what all the commotion was about. The first thing that came to her mind was Jenny, but it had been months since she had been in a fight with a boy. As Melinda ran toward the fight, she could hear shouting and cheering. The children were circled around the two fighting boys and were cheering them on. She gently pushed the children apart so she could walk through. Melinda was so frustrated by this sort of behavior.

"Boys, stop this fighting right now."

The firmness in her voice did not hinder the boys one bit. They ignored her. Melinda tried to pull them apart but couldn't. She didn't have the strength that these hefty boys had. As she pulled and tugged at one of the boys, trying to separate them, he stepped back onto her foot with all of his weight. She let out a gasp as she instantly let go of the boy and backed up, limping in pain. Her foot was throbbing and bruised and she had no way of separating them.

With frustration lacing her voice, she yelled, "Boys, stop fighting this very instant."

The boys still ignored her.

Why were they so angry with one another? She looked around to ask one of the children and she saw Jenny smiling from ear to ear. Why was Jenny smiling? Had she done something to provoke this behavior?

Melinda knelt down beside Jenny and asked, "Do you know anything about this, Jenny?"

"Yup." Jenny grinned.

"Why are these boys fighting?"

Jenny looked into Melinda's eyes and said proudly, "They're fighting over me. Tom gave me a valentine and so did Sam. When Tom found out, he got furious and told Sam that I was his girl and Sam said that I wasn't and that he could give a valentine to any girl he pleased."

Melinda's eyes widened in disbelief. Then she yelled to the boys, "If you don't stop fighting this instant, then you will go home and you won't come back to school for a week."

Instantly, the boys stopped. In the past, they did not mind the chores that Melinda gave them when they acted up, but the last thing they wanted was to be barred from school. What would their parents think? Then Melinda told them that they would stay after school to wash all the desks.

Melinda called the children in from recess. As she walked toward the school, she began to worry that she would run out of jobs for the children to do if they continued with this bad behavior. Why were children so restless when spring approached? Was it the warm air? For these boys, it was infatuation.

Then she thought of Gilbert and began to wonder if he would actually fight for her. Gilbert knew that Henry had been dating her. Hadn't he cared at all? Would he fight for her love as these two young boys had fought for love's sake? Oh, how she wished Gilbert would fight for her!

As the children piled in, Melinda walked to her desk and sat down. She put her elbows on her desk and rested her face in the palm of her hands to relieve the tension. Just then the sound of a broken bottle splattered on the floor. Instantly the room filled with the most putrid, foul, disgusting, detestable odor that Melinda had ever breathed in. The smell was so nauseating and repulsive that it could not be described in words.

The children murmured, "O-o-o-oh yuck! Disgusting!" Then they instantly held their noses with their fingers.

Melinda began to feel sick to her stomach. Her stomach turned over a couple of times before she yelled out, "Children, out of this room quickly before we suffocate from this stench."

The children did not have to process what their teacher told them. It was an instant reflex to jump out of their seats and run out the door for fresh air. Melinda followed the children with her fingers holding tightly to her nose. It seemed as if no one could run fast enough as the children stumbled over one another, racing toward the door.

Melinda gasped in the fresh air as soon as she stepped outside and the nauseating feeling gradually began to leave. The last thing she wanted to see was what she had eaten for breakfast.

After everyone settled down and had taken in some fresh air, Melinda asked, "What was that foul stench?"

Mark looked up at his teacher with embarrassment and said shyly, "It was a bottle of skunk oil, Miss Gamble."

Melinda saw his embarrassment in his reddened face and did not have the heart to scold him when she looked into Mark's pleading eyes.

Billy beamed from ear to ear and said, "Whoa! Miss Gamble, wasn't that something how fast we ran outside after the bottle broke?"

Melinda tried not to chuckle, but she saw the sense of humor in the whole incident. "Well, class, we won't be having school for the rest of the day. I'm going to find Henry so he can clean up inside. My only problem is that I left my purse in the room and I'm not about to go back inside to get it. My stomach couldn't handle it."

Mark looked up at Melinda as if he wanted to be reprieved from his deed. "Miss Gamble, I can hold my breath longer than anyone else. I'll go in to get it for you."

Then he quickly disappeared, running at top speed into the school and back out again. As he came to a stop, he let out a big puff of air. After getting his breath back, he smiled broadly and said, "You see, Miss Gamble, I held my breath the whole time."

Melinda burst out laughing at the funny situation they were all in. This wouldn't have happened in Boston, that was certain! Why hadn't she been aware of what the boys were doing? She smiled at the humor of it and yelled, "Class dismissed."

A cheer rose to high heaven as everyone headed home for the day. Melinda started in the direction of Henry's office. He was in charge of the school grounds and the cleaning of the school. When Melinda brought Henry back to the schoolroom, he became annoyed when he smelled the foul odor from the doorway. The room reeked, to say the least.

"Melinda, it's beyond me what children have in their minds when they bring such things to school. Why don't their parents know what they're doing, anyway?"

"Henry, when you think about it, it's really quite funny. We ran outside faster than a dog chasing a cat." She giggled at the memory of everyone holding their noses and escaping outside, almost stumbling over one another.

"Remember, Melinda, I'll be picking you up at 6:45 tonight. The dance starts at 7:00. Don't be late, all right?"

She smiled. "I'll be ready."

Melinda decided that having a day off was not so bad after all. She needed it desperately. She had plenty to do. Climbing into the carriage, she took off down the road to the Paris Tabernacle. She had been planning to give a spring recital in April and the Tabernacle had the best acoustics.

Melinda was in awe of the beauty of this edifice. It had a steeple that reached into the sky. It was constructed of sandstone and the interior contained the finest woodwork. As Melinda walked inside, she noticed the true artistry of this magnificent building. The sloping floors leading to the podium made it easy to see the speaker or the performer. In front of the podium was a railing that was painted pure white. Behind the podium was another white railing and there were benches for a choir plus a magnificent organ that had been shipped in. The dark wooden organ pipes were set against the wall near the organ. There were balconies on three sides of the room that faced the podium.

The ceiling was rounded, which helped make for fantastic acoustics. The wooden benches in the audience area were smooth and stained a light brown color. The beauty of this Tabernacle was indescribable.

A gentleman walked up to Melinda and greeted her. "Well, hello, Miss Gamble. I hear that you're planning a recital here in April."

"Yes, I am." She waved her hand toward the front of the room. "This building is so beautiful. I was wondering how long it took to build it."

"James Collins was a ship builder and patterned the ceiling after a sailing ship. It took twenty years to gather enough materials to begin construction. Starting in the 1860s, the Mormons gathered wood and quarried sandstone. Then they raised the money to buy what they needed and donated their time to build this Tabernacle, between farming and ranching, that is. It cost them $50,000 and it was completed in 1888."

"How many people can this Tabernacle hold?"

"Fifteen hundred. Come this way, I want to show you something." He pointed to the front doors. "Since hardwood is very expensive, these doors were intricately painted in the graining style to make them look like hardwood."

Melinda eyed the doors and touched them with the palm of her hand. "This looks like it was done by a professional." She was in awe of the beauty of the doors.

After thanking the gentleman, Melinda walked around the outside of this magnificent edifice and stood in awe of the hard work it had taken for these pioneers to build it.

"Beautiful, isn't it, Melinda?"

Melinda recognized that warm deep voice and her spirits soared. She whipped around quickly with a broad smile.

"Gilbert."

Seeing her beautiful smile accelerated Gilbert's heart-beat. He had thought about the things Melinda had told him and he realized she was right. He also realized that he must go on with life. He could not remain in the past. He realized that their differences could complement their relationship. He knew that she did not enjoy cooking, but he did. He did not enjoy gardening, but she did. Her determined attitude helped him to realize that a person should not give up his dreams. Dreams are important in life, and she was his dream. He knew he was in love with Melinda and he realized that he might lose her to Henry if he did not act quickly. He needed to start courting her right away.

"Melinda, I thought you were at school."

"I was until an accident permeated the room. A young boy brought skunk oil to class and you can guess the rest."

"Oh, no." Gilbert cringed. "So you have now been exposed to that despicable odor." He began to chuckle. It was a low, pleasant-sounding chuckle, the kind that would warm a person's soul. "I can't believe it. I'm so sorry for you. How did you fare?"

Melinda noticed how amused he was at her predicament and that made her smile. "My stomach turned over a few times before I realized what was happening."

Gilbert chuckled again. "So, what punishment do you have planned for the little culprit?"

"It was an accident. He didn't have it planned to sabotage the school. I could see in his eyes that he felt bad. So, I just dismissed school for the day until Henry could clean up the mess."

"You're such an understanding woman, Melinda," he said, and then grinned devilishly. "And that's a good job for Henry to do, too. It fits him perfectly."

Melinda looked at Gilbert questioningly as he grinned.

"I heard that you're giving a recital here next month."

Melinda nodded.

"I'll be there for sure." He paused. "I thought I would come by to visit you tonight. Is that all right?"

"Henry's taking me to the dance tonight, Gilbert."

"Oh." A twinge of jealousy shot through him and he tried to ignore it. "How about tomorrow night?"

"I've got a pile of tests that need to be corrected. I planned on correcting them tomorrow night because I had other plans tonight. I'm swamped right now. I'm really sorry but I can't, Gilbert."

"How about Saturday, then?"

"Henry is taking me to dinner in Montpelier."

Gilbert through up his hands in frustration. "Melinda, how far in advance do I need to ask to see you?"

Melinda laughed. "Well, next week I'm practicing with my pianist every evening so we can perfect the songs. But you're invited over for Sunday dinner, I'm sure of it. Aunt Martha loves having you over."

Gilbert felt frustrated. He had been so worried about their differences and about being close to another woman that he had ignored the fact that Melinda was desirable to men other than himself. He had been doing a lot of thinking about her and now he was done thinking. Now it was time for action.

Chapter 23
GILBERT'S DARE

Sunday evening came around and Melinda sat, elated, as she reflected upon a visit from Mark's mother earlier that week. Melinda had been surprised to see her when she showed up at the school. She was a heavyset woman with a sober face.

"Miss Gamble, I want to thank you for not punishing my son for the skunk oil incident. He had gotten into trouble many times with his former teacher just because he doesn't think first. He doesn't mean any harm to others. He just doesn't think before he acts. You're the first teacher who seems to understand him. Thank you. This means a lot to me."

Melinda needed that little boost. She had been feeling a great deal of trepidation, wondering if she had made a difference in anyone's life yet. But as she thought about her goal of doing some good in the world and making a difference in someone's life, she finally realized—with no small amount of amusement—that it was the people here who had made a difference in *her* life. The Wild West and its inhabitants had changed her and she felt that she was a much stronger person than she had been on the first day she arrived. They had strengthened her and she felt more alive, unfettered from the strict conventions of high society. She was able to be herself without worrying about what others would think. The people here were genuine and accepted her without question. She knew that she was a part of this beautiful country now and she could never leave.

As she contemplated the past week, she decided it had been a rewarding week after all. The songs for the recital were coming along quite well and she was feeling satisfied with her accomplishments. Her pianist had been working hard and Melinda was steadily improving on memorization.

When Melinda heard Aunt Martha call her down for Sunday dinner, she quickly descended the stairs and glided gracefully into the kitchen.

Gilbert and Jenny were chatting comfortably at the table. Aunt Martha looked up and said, "I invited guests over for dinner again, Melinda. It seems that Sunday is the only time we get to spend time with you nowadays. Between teaching school and practicing in the evenings, you've been gone every night for the past two weeks, and you've been like a stranger here."

"I'm sorry, Aunt Martha, but it comes to an end this week. Thank goodness."

Melinda cordially greeted Gilbert and Jenny and sat down across from him. Both Gilbert and Melinda knew, uneasily, that even though this was Gilbert's third week in a row at Sunday dinner, they hadn't spent a moment of private time together. Everyone would sit in the living room and talk together and if Gilbert took Melinda for a walk, then Jenny was always tagging along.

Gilbert was the first to speak after the prayer was said and everyone settled down. "Melinda, I saw you a couple times in town during the past week, but you were so busy and intent upon what you were doing that you didn't even notice me. Usually you were headed out of town."

"I'm sorry, Gilbert. My mother always told me that when I go out in pubic I don't seem to notice people as they pass because I'm so absorbed with what I'm doing. My mind seems to be elsewhere nowadays and some of the townsfolk have commented on the fact."

Gilbert chuckled. There was so much he was learning about her and he was enjoying every bit of it. "Your recital is coming up this weekend. What songs are you singing?"

Melinda passed him the potatoes as she answered, "I'm doing a variety of songs. Some Italian, Spanish, English, and Irish. I can't leave out my heritage, you know."

Gilbert grinned and said teasingly, "That's right. How could I ever forget that you're Irish?" Then he began to chuckle warmly.

Everyone looked at Gilbert and seemed to see a sparkle in his eyes and then turned to Melinda. When Melinda noticed everyone was staring at her, she felt warmth creep into her face. Aunt Martha had been teasing her lately about Gilbert and that comment had not helped one bit.

Gilbert noticed her rosy glow and spoke up. "It's sort of a private joke." Then he changed the subject so Melinda would not feel so embarrassed. "Melinda, want to go for a walk after dinner?"

Jenny spoke up excitedly, "Yeah. Let's go."

After clearing the table and doing the dishes, they headed outside for some fresh air. As the three of them strolled in the meadow, Gilbert walked next to Melinda and slipped his hand in hers. She did not seem to mind one bit, and her hand was so warm and soft to the touch.

He suddenly stopped, bent down and picked a wild flower, then turned to Melinda and tucked it behind her ear. She smiled and laughed softly, and he thought she looked so lovely in her white muslin dress. It had puffed sleeves and fit snug to the bodice and hung gracefully about her figure. She had the most delightful laugh and she intrigued him to no end. He noticed how comfortable he felt around her and he just wanted to take her in his arms and hold her, but Jenny was trailing after them and they had no privacy whatsoever. So, he just took her hand in his once again and led her to a stream of water.

Gilbert chuckled and teased her by inviting her to take off her shoes and go wading as she had the first time he met her.

"What did you say, Gilbert?" she asked.

"Do you want to go wading?" He chuckled merrily.

Melinda narrowed her eyes at him. She knew he was daring her in a teasing manner and she was not sure how to respond. When she saw Jenny sitting at the bank and pulling her shoes and socks off, she thought a bit and then she decided to take the dare after all.

Melinda pulled her hand away from his grasp, headed for the stream, and sat down on the bank, slipping off her shoes.

When Gilbert saw what she was doing, he asked, "Are you really going to do it?"

"What do you think, Gilbert?"

"Yeah, Pa," Jenny chimed in with her two cents worth.

When Melinda began to pull her stocking off her leg, Gilbert quickly turned around to give her some privacy. He was surprised that she had taken his dare and he burst into laughter. He was learning more and more about this woman and decided that each thing he learned was absolutely charming.

"What are you laughing at, Gilbert?"

Gilbert's back was to her as he answered, "You took my dare."

After a few seconds, Melinda called out to him, "Ready."

Gilbert turned around and she was already stepping into the water alongside Jenny.

"Come on in, Gilbert. It feels refreshing."

"Yeah, Pa. Come in."

Gilbert shook his head vigorously as he sat down on the bank to relax and watched her intently. He picked a few blades of grass and twirled them between his fingers and stuck another one between his lips. As he watched the two of them walking and talking side by side in the bubbling stream, it brought a smile to Gilbert's lips. Melinda was just like a nymph, free and unfettered from the world. He had never met anyone quite like her.

"Melinda, do you have plans this week? Can I drop by to see you?"

She turned around and looked at Gilbert sitting peace-fully on the bank, he had pulled his knees up and was resting his arms against them, watching her with interest. She smiled and said, "Every evening this week I'll be checking homework or practicing but after the recital I'll be free, no more commitments."

Gilbert nodded, but inside himself he groaned. He had finally made up his mind to court Melinda and now she was constantly busy. Had she cooled off towards him? Was she making up excuses? Had Henry finally won her heart after all before Gilbert had a chance to win it? Had he dragged his feet too long, simply because of his concerns?

For the past week, Gilbert had heard gossip in town about Henry and Melinda from Henry's friends and family. Henry's brother said, "Henry told me that he's going to ask Melinda to marry him right after her recital, that very night. They've been dating for four months now. He's ready to settle down."

Gilbert remembered how his face had reddened with a mixture of jealousy and disgust that stirred within him. Without saying a word, he had walked out of the barbershop and headed for home. He was beside himself with worry. Why had he waited so long to realize that he wanted to marry Melinda? Was it too late? Would she accept Henry's proposal on Saturday?

Gilbert had not taken the time to court her and he did not count Sunday dinners and walks—with Jenny tagging along—as a courtship. To him, when a man went courting, he would take her to someplace special and then end the evening with a romantic kiss. The only time he had kissed Melinda was at the terminal and that did not constitute a legal goodnight kiss, even though it was one of the most romantic kisses he had ever felt in his life. That kiss had stirred feelings within him that he thought were dormant and it made him begin to think about his future.

After Jenny and Melinda hopped out of the stream, they sat down on the bank. Melinda dried their feet with her petticoats before slipping on their stockings and shoes.

Gilbert stood and helped Jenny up from the bank. She cried out in excitement as she ran toward the house to tell Aunt Martha about the fun they had had. As Gilbert watched her run off, he breathed a sigh of relief. Maybe he could now have a little private time with Melinda after all. He held his hand out to Melinda and helped her to her feet.

"Why did you take my dare?"

Melinda smiled. "I don't know."

Gilbert grinned at her. "Come on. Why did you?"

"Well, I love wading, as you well know."

"No, why did you take my dare? I saw you hesitating when I asked if you wanted to go wading. And you knew I was teasing you."

She looked down at the ground. "As I think about it, I believe it was because of Jenny. When I saw her taking off her shoes, I guess I wanted to be close to her. I guess that I wanted to do something fun with her." She looked up into his eyes. "You know, I'd like a relationship beyond the classroom, where I didn't represent her teacher. I don't know if I make any sense or not."

"Why was that important to you?"

Melinda looked surprised. As she looked into his piercing dark eyes, she smiled. "Because I love her."

This answer took him by surprise. No other teacher had ever shown this kind of love for Jenny before. "Why do you love her, Melinda?"

"She's easy to love, Gilbert."

Gilbert smiled in agreement, not saying a word.

His eyes looked deeply into hers, searching them and wondering what her true feelings were for him. Then he stepped forward, took her firmly by the shoulders and pulled her close to him, kissing her tenderly upon the lips, lingering longer than he expected. He had never been so impulsive before, but with Melinda, he seemed like a different person.

The love he felt for this woman was undeniable. For the first time in eight years, he was truly in love. The happiness he felt when he was around her was indescribable. This woman had changed his life for the better and she did not even know it. But what surprised him the most was that she immediately wrapped her arms around his neck, stood on her toes, and kissed him right back with a passion he had not expected that sent a tingle down his spine. She never ceased to amaze him. She was never one to hide her feelings and it made his heart race with even greater love for this amazingly tender and sensitive woman. Did she know the effects she was having on him? Melinda's influence had made him want to become a better person. Each day he felt greater happiness than he had ever felt before, and it was all because of her. Had he done something right, after all, for God to reward him with such a treasure?

Chapter 24
THE RECITAL

By April, rains were warming the ground and a few flowers began to pop out of the earth. Spring was on its way. The ground was like a beautiful green carpet of grass and weeds. Leaves were budding and waving with the breeze.

On the evening of the recital, it seemed that everyone was excited about the event. Friends and neighbors showed up, along with many strangers from neighboring towns such as Montpelier. Henry sat in the front row and Gilbert sat in the middle section with Jenny.

Melinda was wearing a white silk dress with puffed sleeves to her elbows. The neckline was rounded and trimmed with lace and the dress was gathered just below the bust. Behind her was a lovely train that trailed after her as she walked. Her hair was placed loosely upon her head with ringlets cascading over the combs in the back, and a red flower was pinned in her hair. Around her slender neck she wore simple pearls.

Melinda opened her recital with a lively Spanish song that created a cheerful mood for the evening. Her voice was rich and beautiful. Each note and word that she sang delighted and lifted the spirits of everyone there. It seemed as if she were singing from the depths of her heart.

Gilbert relaxed as he listened to each melodic note she sang and his heart swelled within him as she came upon the climax of each song. Each piece had a message, and he felt what she was saying through her notes and emotions. When she finally sang a love song, he noticed that she glanced at him quite often and he felt as if she were singing to him. His pulse picked up speed as he listened to each word she sang, and he wondered if she really was singing to him.

The evening came to a close with a melancholy Irish song that touched the hearts of the audience and brought tears to many. The mellow sound of her voice expressed a message of love. When she gave a bow, the applause was heartfelt and it touched Melinda's soul.

After the recital, Gilbert noticed a long line of people waiting to shake Melinda's hand and thank her for the lovely evening. He also noticed Henry standing at the end of the line with a broad smile on his face and a bunch of flowers in his hand. Gilbert knew that he would ask Melinda to marry him after the recital.

What would Melinda's answer be? They had been dating for some time and she probably would like to settle down. She was past the age that women usually married, so why wouldn't she accept such an offer? Henry had a good, secure job and the townsfolk seemed to think that she would accept his offer. There would be no reason to refuse.

Gilbert's heart felt heavy and he could not approach her. If he shook her hand, he knew his heart would skip a beat and then what would he do? He had not even had a chance to court her and now she was receiving an offer of marriage that very night. Sadness overtook him and he felt heartsick. Gilbert's chest felt tight as he took Jenny's hand, and they walked out of the building without a word.

When Melinda saw Gilbert and Jenny leave, she wondered why they did not stand in line to talk to her. Perhaps they had something pressing afterwards. What else could it be? Maybe he would stop off at the house later and tell her what he thought.

When the Tabernacle had been cleared of people, Henry took Melinda aside and proposed to her. Melinda was expecting it because she, like everyone else, had heard the gossip in town.

When Henry gave her the flowers and proposed, she smiled warmly and said with kindness and warmth in her voice, "Henry, you're a very sweet person and I like you a lot. But we've already talked about this before, remember? We're friends and that's all it can be. The fact is that you would be a perfect match for me. You believe in education for women. You have stated the fact that I could continue teaching after marriage, and you definitely believe in equality for women. You're not opinionated or stubborn like most men I've met. In fact, you're everything a woman would want, but…"

When Henry noticed her hesitation, he asked, "But what, Melinda? Tell me."

"I'm sorry, Henry, but when I marry it will be for love. That's important to me."

Clearly disappointed, he asked, "Melinda, do you love someone else? Is that it?"

Melinda hesitated for a moment, looking down at the floor and biting her lip. "Yes, I do."

Henry stood a while in thought, as if wondering how he could defeat his rival. "That's all I wanted to know, Melinda, because if you didn't love another, I wouldn't give up. But I guess its time to bow out, isn't it?" He gave a crooked smile and said quietly in a defeated manner, "Good luck, Melinda. I hope he loves you, too."

Henry turned to leave, but Melinda touched his arm and he turned and looked into her eyes.

"Henry, I've loved the times we've had lunch together at school. It was fun to sit and talk each day while the kids went out to eat. Please, we're still friends, aren't we? I don't want to lose you as a dear friend. We've had good times, you know. Very good times."

Henry smiled and nodded. "That we have."

"Henry, are you still going to bring your lunch to school so we can eat together, like usual?"

Henry nodded and touched her cheek gently. Then it came to him. He would treat her like everything was all right, hoping he still had a chance to win her over. Surely an educated gentleman had a better chance than an uneducated cattle rancher. "I'd love to still have lunch with you every day. This doesn't change anything."

"Thank you, Henry. I still need a friend, you know."

"I know."

Melinda wrapped her arms around him and gave him a hug before sending him on his way. After he left, Melinda thought about what he had said: "I hope he loves you, too."

She truly didn't know whether Gilbert loved her or not. He had never said. All she knew was that he was afraid of their differences and had told her so at the Valentine's Dance. She knew that he liked her, but she was certain he was afraid of commitment.

She gathered her skirts and slowly walked toward the front door. She stopped on the step just outside the door and gazed thoughtfully into the night sky, noticing the brightness of the stars above. She gave a sigh as she thought of her quandary. This was the first time she had fallen in love and she had to fall for someone who was afraid to commit to a relationship. What a dilemma!

Chapter 25
FISHING

Two weeks had passed since Melinda's recital and Gilbert had continuously heard from Jenny how happy Melinda was. Jenny had told him how Henry would bring his lunch to school and they would sit and eat together in the classroom during lunchtime. Then she told him how she laughed at Henry's jokes as they ate and how jovial they sounded together.

Jenny hoped to spark something in her father by telling him this news so he would not dilly-dally any longer and start to court Melinda. She hoped that he would get a little jealous and then do something about it, like fight for the woman he loved. Her father was dragging his feet and she thought she could help him along.

But unbeknownst to her, Jenny's gossip created just the opposite effect. Gilbert assumed that the friendliness and joviality between Melinda and Henry indicated that she had actually accepted Henry's proposal. After all, what man in his right mind would continue a relationship with a woman if he had been refused by her? And Gilbert knew, begrudgingly, that Melinda and Henry had so much in common. Defeated, Gilbert avoided going to town because he did not want to hear about their engagement. He kept busy on his ranch and Jenny worked beside him, as usual.

Gilbert's heart ached. How could he have lost someone as dear to him as she was? Why had he been so cautious and dimwitted? He was a fool. He knew he had lost his heart to her when he had picked her up at the terminal in January and yet he did not act upon it. She had responded to his tender kiss both times he kissed her, and she would have accepted his proposal. He knew that now. Was it too late? Would he still have a chance to win her over? Could he steal her away from Henry without the town looking down upon him? He had never felt such deep love for someone as he did for Melinda. No, he had to remove Melinda from his memory because he ached too deeply inside just knowing that he had lost her to another.

Suddenly a loud noise came from the kitchen, jolting him out of his thoughts. Jenny had tied a couple of strings to two black pans and then tied them to her feet, clomping around the kitchen. Each pan came down with a loud thud until Gilbert demanded, "Enough! Enough! Cease and desist! No more noise, Jenny."

That ended the fun for Jenny and she put away the pans. She noticed that her father had been moping around the house lately and that he seemed extra grumpy. It did not take long for Jenny to see that she needed to do something about it.

"Pa, I'm taking you out of this house. What do you want to do?"

"Nothing. I'll be all right soon. Don't worry about me. I've just been working hard and I'm tired. That's all."

"I know what to do. You have promised to take me fishing for the longest time and you haven't. You said you would teach me how to fish. How about it, Pa?"

Gilbert smiled at his daughter. He realized that he had not been in the best of spirits and he needed to change all that.

"All right, Jenny, get my fishing gear. We'll pack up some sandwiches and we'll go. First, we'll dig us some worms."

"Thanks, Pa."

Jenny was not really interested in fishing, but she had to do something to get her father out of the house. He seemed to be working extra hard lately and he needed some free time from his chores and the ranch. She could not figure out what was bothering him. He had seemed extra moody ever since her teacher's recital. She knew that he loved to fish and perhaps this would settle him down.

Gilbert and Jenny saddled their horses and took off toward Bear Lake. As they rode, they talked. When Jenny brought up school and Miss Gamble, she noticed that her father would quickly change the subject, which was unusual. He always seemed interested when she talked about her education before.

"Hey Pa, why don't we go see Miss Gamble and invite her to go fishing with us?"

Gilbert was taken aback by this suggestion and he quickly blurted out, "We're not going to Martha's home anymore, Jenny, and certainly not to see Miss Gamble."

"Why not?"

"Because she's busy with other matters at this time. No more discussion, all right? We're going fishing and we're going to have a good time. Got it?"

"No, I don't get it, Pa. Why can't we see Miss Gamble any more?"

"Because Henry wouldn't like it."

"Heck with Henry, Pa. Why don't you fight for her?"

Gilbert looked over at her in surprise and asked, "What did you say?"

"I said to fight for her," she said as she swung a fist in the air with determination. "Tom and Sam fought for me and that made me realize who really cared. Sam wouldn't let Tom tell him what to do, so he fought for me."

Gilbert stared at her with concern. "You had two boys fight over you?"

"Sure, Pa. Don't you think Miss Gamble is worth it?" She gave another punch in the air for emphasis while holding tight to the reins with her other hand.

"It's different in this situation, darlin'. Completely different."

"Well, at least think about it. All right, Pa?"

Gilbert looked out toward the beautiful lake they were approaching, and said, "I'll think about it."

When they arrived at Bear Lake, Gilbert taught Jenny how to put a worm on her hook. Jenny cringed as she followed his instructions.

When Gilbert saw Jenny wrinkle her nose as she shoved the worm on the hook, he grinned. This was exactly what he needed. He enjoyed fishing because it was so relaxing. Being with his daughter was the perfect therapy for what ailed him. She was the most important part of his life and he adored her beyond explanation.

Gilbert noticed a few splashes in the water where the fish were lunging for flies and mosquitoes; the fish were biting. He taught Jenny how to throw her line into the water and then he threw in his hook. Jenny sat beside him on the bank, holding her rod. She sat still, but not one fish seemed interested in her bait. After a while, she became bored and wondered why her father loved this sport so much.

Gilbert swished his pole from side to side to get their attention and it was not long until a fish grabbed the moving worm on his hook. When he felt the fish tug at the line, he slowly reeled it in. The fish struggled and struggled with all its might as Gilbert pulled on his line. He had to keep the line taut so this nimble little fish would not get away. After a while, he had it hanging in the air from his rod. Gilbert grabbed the line with his left hand and looked at the fish with a grin.

"Now this is a fine fish!"

Gilbert was very excited as he eyed his catch. He had never caught a fish that large before.

Jenny watched with interest, wondering what her father was going to do next. She saw him carefully take the hook out of the fish's mouth. She saw the fish wiggling and wiggling as her father put it in a small bucket. As she watched the fish wiggle, sadness overtook her. Before long, her eyes filled up with tears. Her heart pounded loudly as big drops of tears began to fall down her cheeks.

Jenny looked up at her father and begged, "Pa, put him back in the water."

Gilbert was busy putting another fat worm on his hook when he heard her voice quiver. He turned to look at her and saw tears trickling down her cheeks. He became confused. Jenny was the one who had begged to go fishing in the first place.

"Pa, the fish is suffering. See him wiggling and trying to fight for his life. He wants to go back to his family. How would you like it if someone took me away from you? Pa, he wants to live his life and be happy. See? He's suffering. Please let him go."

Gilbert watched the tears fall down Jenny's cheeks. He wrapped his arm around her and held her tight and wiped her tears away with his handkerchief. Then she looked at her father with questioning eyes, and touched his hand gently.

That was it! Gilbert could not resist those blue eyes. He looked into the bucket and stared at his catch. Then he grabbed the fish and threw it back into the water.

Jenny wrapped her arms around her father's waist and gave him a hug. "Thanks, Pa. Thank you so much."

"It's the biggest fish I've ever caught, but it's all right. I wasn't in the mood for fish, anyway. By the way, did you know that God made fish for us to eat?"

"Yes, I know, Pa. But I just couldn't stand watching him suffer so."

"I understand." He wiped a tear from her cheek and said, "Let's go back home and have some cookies instead."

"All right, Pa." Jenny leaped up excitedly with a smile. "I'm sorry for ruining your fun."

"Don't worry, sweetheart. You're more important to me than the largest fish I've ever caught in my life."

Jenny began swatting mosquitoes that were landing on her arms and neck and she became annoyed by their persistence to have her for supper.

Gilbert noticed the pesky mosquitoes and said, "Maybe it's time to go home, anyway. The mosquitoes must think your blood is sweet."

The following day, Gilbert decided to go to the school and confront the situation and do as Jenny had suggested— fight for Melinda's love. So, he climbed into his saddle and rode to the schoolhouse. As he rode along, he tried to memorize a speech that would sound convincing, educated, and not emotional. After arriving, he found that Melinda was not there and had dismissed school early that day.

"She left about an hour ago, Gilbert," said Henry with a smug look on his face. "Besides, if you need to talk to her about your child, you don't come during school hours. You make an appointment. Got it?"

He was firm and abrupt with his answer. It was clear that Henry wasn't happy to see Gilbert there.

Gilbert took a deep breath, trying to keep his cool, and asked, "Where did she go? Is she home?"

"That's none of your business, Gilbert."

Gilbert took another deep breath and tried again. "I know you don't like me, Henry. But Melinda has a right to choose whether or not she wants to speak to me."

Henry slammed his hand on the desk for emphasis. "She wants nothing to do with you, Gilbert. Leave her alone."

Henry was trying Gilbert's patience to the very limits and Gilbert was having a tough time enduring his unfriendly attitude.

Henry glared at Gilbert as he said, "And if you want to make an appointment with her to speak about Jenny, I'll be glad to do that for you."

Gilbert turned to leave. He had had enough of this man's ornery attitude. Just as he got to the entrance of the schoolroom, he turned and asked, "So when's the date?"

"What date?"

"Of your marriage."

Henry grinned. "That's none of your business." He walked up to Gilbert and stood up close to his face, as if daring him to challenge him. "Remember, Melinda's my girl, not yours." Then with a haughty attitude, he gave Gilbert a firm shove out the door.

That was it. Gilbert had kept his cool long enough. Without another word, he stepped forward and took a swing at Henry that landed right on his nose. Henry stumbled backwards, landing on a student's desk with a surprised look on his face as he held his bleeding nose with his hand.

Then Gilbert turned and abruptly walked away. This was not what he had planned. He had planned a perfect speech to convince her of his love and now he had just battered the man she was going to marry. Why had he lost his temper? She would never see him again after this fiasco. Why hadn't he just gone to her home instead of confronting Henry? After hearing about this incident, she would be ashamed to speak to him.

Gilbert stomped off toward his horse, hopped on, and rode out of town, feeling completely defeated.

Chapter 26
A MISUNDERSTANDING

Two and a half weeks passed after Melinda's recital and still she heard no word from Gilbert. She had invited him to call on her after the recital and he had not done so, and it appeared that he never would. Melinda's emotions were on the edge and she wanted to cry. Gilbert seemed to be avoiding her. Aunt Martha had invited him over twice for Sunday dinner, and he had refused both times, saying he was too busy. It was not like Gilbert to refuse a meal. What was wrong? If Gilbert was not avoiding her, then what was his real excuse for not coming to dinner? When Melinda asked Jenny about her father's absence, her answer came as quite a surprise.

"We weren't busy, Miss Gamble. We didn't do a thing but sit around and read. He didn't even tell me that we were invited over to your house for dinner." Jenny lowered her head in despair and continued, "Also, Pa said that we wouldn't be visiting you any longer and I'm not sure why. He seems so moody lately."

The following day, Melinda excused class early so she could help Aunt Martha take Uncle William to the doctor in Montpelier. When she went back later to get some tests she had forgotten to grade, she met Henry. His nose was red and swollen and he had stuffed a handkerchief up one nostril. He was quite a sight.

When she inquired about what happened to his nose, he said in a most innocent manner, "You want to know what happened? I'll tell ya what happened. Your boyfriend confronted me. He just walked in here and picked a fight with me. And I didn't do a thing to provoke him. He punched me for no reason whatsoever. He's not the man for you, Melinda. He's got a violent temper. When I told him to leave, he just up and slugged me. You wouldn't be happy with such a fellow. You need someone that'll be gentle with you." He hesitated for a moment and then said, "Like me."

Melinda was shocked. This was not the Gilbert she had gotten to know. He was not violent. She was very confused by the idea of him punching Henry without provocation.

Melinda decided to take a walk and think. She had only one month left of school and then she would return to Boston for the summer and not see Gilbert for three months. And when she returned, would he still avoid her? Were his concerns that he expressed during the Valentine's Dance still bothering him? If he still felt the same way, her heart would break and she would not be able to bear to see him while he felt indifferent towards her. The memory of his kiss lingered within her and she could not get it out of her mind.

Maybe, just maybe, she should not renew her contract after all. Maybe this western life wasn't for her. Her heart was aching inside and her chest was tight and full of emotion. Maybe walking would help her feel better. If she did not feel better after this walk, then she would write a letter of resignation to the school board and she would not return in the fall.

One thing continued to bother her most of all: Gilbert had not told Melinda whether or not he had enjoyed her recital. The recital meant a lot to her; she had worked tirelessly, and he had not gone out of his way to tell her what he had thought about it. Were they not friends, at least? She resolved not to think about it any longer and knew if she walked among nature, she would feel better. In fact, she thought, she could not wait to return to Boston after all.

As Melinda walked through the thick grove of quaking aspens and pines, she noticed a squirrel scampering toward a tree and climbing as fast as its little feet could go. Melinda was amused as she came over the hill and around a bend, her eyes still glued on the scampering squirrel. Not looking where she was going, she bumped into an object. It was not an inanimate object, though. This object happened to be human. She had stumbled right into Gilbert and he caught her by the arms as they collided.

With a look of shock and surprise on his face, he exclaimed, "Melinda!" Catching his breath, he saw that he had startled her as well and he asked, "Are you all right?"

After getting her breath back, Melinda abruptly pulled herself away from his grasp. She felt hurt, angry, and saddened, and with all of this meshed into one emotion, she snapped at him.

"No, I'm not."

Gilbert was surprised by her attitude and his eyes widened in disbelief. "What's wrong, Melinda?" he asked as he saw her stiffen. He noticed that her eyes were unreadable and her attitude was cool.

"You don't know?"

"Are you angry because of what happened between me and Henry?" he asked with caution.

"Of course not. That has nothing to do with me. That's between you and Henry."

"Then why are you ornery with me? Have I done something wrong?"

"Have you done something wrong? Now that's an understatement. Yes, you have. I thought we were friends." When Melinda's eyes began to moisten against her will, she turned her head so Gilbert would not notice.

"We are, Melinda."

Gilbert's eyes searched her face for an answer. If she was not upset about the little fiasco he had had with Henry, then why did she sound so upset? Her attitude definitely confused him.

"Well, friends don't forget one another, especially during a special time."

Gilbert's heart began to throb with pain. He was in agony. Didn't she understand how deep his feelings were for her? The turmoil of the last couple of weeks had been difficult for him.

Trying to hide his feelings from her, he said solemnly, "Oh, yes. Congratulations. I'm sorry I didn't tell you sooner. I haven't gone into town for a couple weeks."

"Congratulations? For what? I was talking about my recital. You didn't tell me how I did and what you thought about it. That was a special time for me because I hadn't sung here before and I was excited to do so. I worked very hard and it was important to me, but you didn't even care to say a word about it to me. Right after the recital you disappeared and I haven't seen you since."

Gilbert's heart was aching and his features were laced with pain. Standing in front of Melinda like this was very hard. All he wanted to do was enfold her in his arms one more time. She was so achingly beautiful. But he listened as she spoke.

"And another thing, why didn't you come over for Sunday dinner? You never refuse a meal. Are you avoiding me?"

Melinda's frustration was obvious. Her eyes continued to moisten and that frustrated her even more. She did not want Gilbert to see her become emotional. She blinked back the tears and waited for an answer.

"Yes, I was avoiding you."

Melinda was so hurt by his answer that she quickly turned her head and looked toward the mountains, trying very hard to blink back the tears that stung her eyes. Her hands began to tremble with anxiety and the pain in her heart intensified.

"Melinda, I didn't accept the dinner invitation because I figured Henry wouldn't like it."

Her head jerked back and she faced him with confusion in her eyes. "What does Henry have to do with all this?"

Gilbert took a deep breath, trying to muster up the courage to tell her how he felt. "Melinda, if you were my fiancée, I would not like it at all if you had dinner with Henry. In fact, I wouldn't even like it if I knew you two met in the woods like this, especially if I knew what was in his heart." He paused. "If he knew what was in my heart, Melinda, he wouldn't like it."

Gilbert knew exactly what was in his own heart. Could Henry possibly feel as deeply for a woman as he did for Melinda? How he loved this woman standing in front of him! If she only knew how it broke his heart to stand before her like this, longing to hold her in his arms once again, what would she think?

"Fiancée? Heart?" Melinda burst out with emotion. Her frustration elevated and she was confused, not to mention perturbed by his statement. Her throat became constricted as she spoke. "Did you say fiancée? I couldn't marry Henry. I'm not in love with him." She shook her head in exasperation. "How could I marry Henry when I'm in love with another? You are such a fool, Gilbert."

Then she turned on her heels and quickly marched away with tears trickling down her cheeks. Her hands were trembling and her heart pounded furiously. She wiped the tears away with her sleeve but they persisted to form beyond her control.

Gilbert was at a loss for words. She stormed off, leaving him with his mouth wide open in surprise. What did she mean that she was in love with another? He watched her as she took off with long and quick strides, the distance widening between them. He shook his head in frustration and quickly ran after her. Just as she was heading down the slope, he caught up to her and grabbed her firmly around the arm to stop her.

Looking into her eyes, he asked, "Did you say you weren't engaged to Henry?"

"Yes, Gilbert. I did. Now let go of me and leave me alone."

Her voice had an edge to it and Gilbert could see that she was not in the mood to talk anymore. Melinda struggled to pull herself away from his firm grasp. Her frustration slowly began to leave and was replaced with sorrow.

As she struggled to pull away, he held her tightly by the arm and asked in a tender voice, "Who are you in love with, Melinda?"

She turned to face him and answered impatiently, "Are you so oblivious of my feelings, Gilbert? Don't you know? Can't you tell how I feel about you?"

She struggled out of his grasp as he stood motionless with surprise written all over his face. This was not what he had expected at all. Her bluntness, to be sure, was even more shocking. She had come right to the point and said what she felt and his heart began to swell within him.

Gilbert noticed that Melinda was walking at a very fast pace and he ran to catch up to her. As he dashed in front of her, she came to a stop. Then he took her by the shoulders with both hands and said, "Don't be so stubborn, Melinda. Listen to me. Please listen. Give me a chance to explain. All right?"

Melinda averted her eyes so he could not see the pain inside them. The last thing she wanted was for him to feel pity for her.

Gilbert tried to look into her eyes and he saw the sorrow within them. She could not hide it sufficiently from one who knew her so well. It pained him deeply to see her feel this way and he groaned inside himself. He needed to finally tell her how he felt about her. There was no time to wait for a proper courtship. She needed to know right now without any hesitation.

"Melinda, listen to me." When he saw that she was avoiding eye contact, he decided to go a different direction. "So, I guess I slugged an innocent man all for nothing, didn't I?"

That got her attention right away, and she turned to face him. "What?"

"Melinda, I didn't talk to you the night of the recital because I knew Henry was proposing to you that night. You had been dating for some time and I thought you might accept. I couldn't face you, knowing this."

"Why not, Gilbert?" Melinda looked up into his eyes with intensity, waiting for an answer, the right answer.

"Because of my own feelings for you, Melinda. For the longest time I've tried to deny my deep feelings for you. Then when I realized that I needed you in my life, I thought it was too late. When I thought I'd lost you to another, I couldn't bear it. I ached inside just thinking that you belonged to Henry. That's when Jenny opened my eyes and told me that I needed to fight for you. So, I went to the school yesterday and confronted Henry. But I guess I hit an innocent man, didn't I?"

When he saw the surprised look in her eyes, he smiled. "Melinda, my heart is so full of love for you. There is no other woman in this world for me but you." Gilbert saw her eyes widen and her mouth open slightly. He smiled at her, amused at her expression. "Did you hear me, Melinda? I have fallen in love with you. The day I saw you wading in that stream and heard you laughing so delightfully, I knew I was going to lose my heart. But I tried to guard it so carefully and I shouldn't have."

Melinda's features softened as she looked into his eyes and asked, "You actually fought for me, Gilbert?"

"Uh-huh. But I'm afraid it didn't go well at all. I didn't mean to hurt him. I was afraid you were mad at me for what happened."

"You fought for me?" she asked once again in disbelief.

Gilbert grinned as he took a handkerchief from his pocket, dabbed the wetness from her cheeks, and continued, "Melinda, I fell for your charm, your honesty, your determination, your independence, and your intelligence. I fell for your frankness and boldness to say what was on your mind. And yes, I even fell in love with your stubbornness and your strong self-will. There isn't a thing about you that I'm not in love with. I even love the way we argue together."

Melinda's eyes began to glow with each word, more so from the tone of his voice than from the words he said.

While he put his handkerchief back in his pocket, Gilbert chuckled softly as he watched a smile gradually appear upon her lips. He slid his hands around her waist and embraced her in his arms and held her for the longest time while she leaned her head against his shoulder. As he squeezed her tightly against his chest with the palms of his hands, he felt her respond to his touch and melt into his arms with a soft sigh.

Gilbert snuggled his cheek next to hers and he whispered into her ear, "Besides, Melinda, I just love the way you melt into my arms and respond to my hugs. It makes me want to hold you forever. When we're apart, it seems as if my life isn't complete. All I do is think about you and how much I love you." He took a deep breath and let it out slowly. "Will you marry me, Melinda?"

Melinda's heart fluttered and her pulse raced as she listened to every word he said. His warm breath against her ear sent tingles down her spine. Her spirits soared and she did not want to come back down to earth again. She could not imagine being happier than she was at this very moment. Just hearing his voice telling her of his love was all she needed to send her spirits soaring. The touch of his hands against her back made her heart sing. His arms were strong and warm and protective. Happiness flooded through her and she wondered if this were a dream, if this were what fairy tales were like.

Then she remembered her mother's words: "The kind of love you're expecting only happens in fairy tales. Are you waiting for a knight in shining armor to save you from a ferocious beast and take you into his arms and then ride off together on his white horse?"

Yes, he was her knight in shining armor and he had actually saved her from a ferocious beast and a blinding blizzard. The thought of him in shining armor made her grin.

While she was cradled in his arms, he said softly, "Please tell me you'll marry me, Melinda."

Then he pulled back to look into her eyes and she smiled and slowly nodded. "Yes, Gilbert, I will. I realized I had fallen in love with you when you kissed my hand at Christmastime. During my whole vacation, I kept thinking about you and comparing other men to you and no one seemed to measure up. There was no one else who had your qualities. And then, when you kissed me at the terminal, I realized I had lost my heart to you." She looked lovingly into his eyes and said, "Besides, Gilbert, didn't you see that I was singing that love song to you at my recital? I thought you noticed that I was looking at you and singing only to you. Didn't you notice?"

As Gilbert listened, he searched her face and eyes and his heart skipped a beat. He knew at that very moment he would love her, not for just a lifetime, but for all eternity.

"Yes, I noticed, Melinda."

Gilbert's eyes trailed down to her mouth as he pulled her close to his chest and touched his warm lips to hers. He kissed her with such tenderness that warmth crept into her rosy cheeks and traveled down to the tips of her toes. The heat from his kiss began to envelop her from the inside out and happiness overtook her. His kiss was one of tenderness and longing. It was the most romantic and passionate kiss she had ever felt in her life.

Melinda knew that Gilbert had the purest love for her: unconditional love. She knew that Gilbert loved her unconditionally and this impressed her so much. He was not judgmental of her. He accepted her for who she was. Gilbert had let her know that her strong self-will and stubborn attitude were assets rather than weaknesses. Because of his unconditional love, Melinda felt their love could rise above any love in history.

When he finally released her, she looked into his eyes and asked once again, "Did you really fight for me?"

"Well, in a way. I really went there for the sole purpose of convincing you to marry me and not Henry."

Melinda smiled. "I've never had anyone fight for me before, Gilbert."

"Then you're in for a real treat because I'll never let you go ever again."

Chapter 27
THE LAST TEST

A month passed quickly. Gilbert and Jenny whistled merrily as they cleaned the house to prepare for his wedding, which was the following morning. They wanted the house to be perfectly clean for Melinda's arrival to her new home. Gilbert swept as Jenny dusted.

"Pa?"

"Yes, dear?"

"I don't know what to call Miss Gamble when you get married tomorrow. Should I call her Ma or Mama, or should I just call her what you call her—Melinda?"

"Whatever makes you feel the most comfortable, darlin'."

"Yesterday when I saw Miss Gamble, she told me that she loved me the very first time she saw me." Jenny's eyes began to moisten. "I asked her why she did and she said to me, 'Do you remember what I wrote on the board the first day of school?' And I told her that I did. And she said

'Jenny, I loved you more because you needed it more.'
Then she said that she knew I was special from the first
time she saw me." Jenny's voice cracked and tears formed
in her eyes and she could not speak.

Gilbert took a handkerchief out of his pocket and knelt
down beside Jenny and wiped her cheeks dry. "So it was
her love that won you. Is that right, Jenny?"

"Yes, Pa. She loved me even when I caused her bunches
of trouble. I knew I was causing trouble, Pa, but I hated
those boys and I didn't care if it disrupted the class or not.
She even loved me when I wouldn't do my lessons at
school and she said it was all right and she was patient with
me until I was ready to do my lessons."

"Hmm, so you gave your new teacher heartaches?"

"Yes, Pa. I did."

Gilbert chuckled as he stuffed his handkerchief in his
pocket. Then he kissed Jenny on the cheek and hugged her.
Just then he heard a knock on the door, which disturbed
their tender moment. When Jenny opened it, Martha
walked in carrying a large bundle in her arms and a broad
smile on her face.

"Gilbert, I have made this wedding present for you. It's
a feather quilt for your bed so that your new wife won't get
cold."

Gilbert grinned at Martha and teasingly said, "Don't
worry about that, Martha. It's *my* responsibility to keep her
warm at night. She's so cuddly that I won't let go of her,
I'm afraid."

Martha blushed and reprimanded him teasingly. "Gilbert!"

"Oh, Martha, don't act so innocent. You had this planned all along. Remember that mistletoe?"

Martha acted innocent as usual and replied, "I don't know what you're talking about, Gilbert."

"Martha, don't play coy with me. I saw you set up the snack table right next to the doorway in the kitchen. I knew what you were doing. You didn't fool me one bit."

Martha grinned. "Well, I had to do something. You certainly weren't. You seemed to be too busy to court her."

"No, I wasn't too busy, Martha. I was scared. It was fear that overtook me."

"Fear? But you're so tough. I wouldn't think that such a tough man would ever feel scared about anything."

Gilbert grinned at her compliment. "Martha, even tough guys get scared."

"Were you afraid of Melinda? When I noticed that you wouldn't kiss her beneath the mistletoe, I should have realized it."

"Oh, no, Martha. You're wrong. I wasn't afraid of Melinda. I wanted to kiss her very much. I wanted to take her in my arms and kiss her more than you know but when I looked into her eyes that night, I could tell she wasn't ready. She blushed and she had a timid look in her eyes and I realized that I couldn't embarrass her. Nor could I back down after you pointed out the mistletoe. She would think I didn't like her at all and that would be even worse than embarrassing her. So, I just kissed her hand."

"Then what were you afraid of, Gilbert?"

"Myself. I was afraid of what I would do to this precious person. I didn't want to ruin her life. Melinda was an Eastern lady and I was a rancher. I thought the two wouldn't mix. Before I married my first wife, she was full of enthusiasm. She laughed all the time and seemed so happy until we got married. I thought she stopped laughing because I had forced her to live in a country that was not yet tame. But at the Valentine's Dance, Melinda helped me to understand myself better. She explained how differences are important. I had to stop blaming myself for my wife's death, too. After a few weeks of thinking, I began to realize that Melinda had gone through a lot of tests while living here and she had passed them all. And she still wanted to come back to teach school in the fall. I began to think that she wasn't such a tenderfoot after all."

"What tests are you referring to, Gilbert?"

"Oh, she experienced a bank robbery by the notorious Butch Cassidy. Then she encountered a grizzly bear that was more terrifying than you or I could ever imagine. Not to mention all the rest of her inner turmoil over being a teacher and taking on all the fun experiences such as skunk oil and rowdy children." Gilbert began to chuckle at the thought of skunk oil. "So, you see, Martha, I had to work all this out in my mind first before I could court her. Then the next fear I had was that she had accepted Henry's proposal. That was my greatest fear of all. You don't know how much I anguished inside and suffered after thinking she was engaged to him. I even blamed myself for being such a fool."

"Well, if you would have let Melinda go back home this summer, then you would have been."

Gilbert chuckled warmly. That was a fact and he knew it. And if she had gone home, he would have gone after her all the way to Boston.

After Martha went home, she found Melinda in the most cheerful mood. Melinda's heart soared as she remembered how Gilbert had asked Uncle William for her hand in marriage since her father was not around. School was over, and she was preparing for her wedding day. Melinda was so excited. Her parents would arrive tomorrow morning for the wedding and life could not be more perfect.

Melinda could not sit still, so she decided to take one last afternoon walk before her wedding day. It was May and the air smelled fresh as she strolled toward the mountains. She felt a slight breeze sift through her hair and brush across her cheeks.

As she walked toward the woods, she watched the crystal water running down from the mountain over stones and rocks. It shimmered and sparkled in the sunlight and joy overtook her. The sound of it was soothing and lulling to her nerves. A carpet of yellow and white wildflowers was blooming on every side of the valley and a sweet fragrance was in the air. The sunshine was pleasant on her shoulders and she could see the hand of God in every blade of grass, leaf, tree, and bud. Colorful butterflies emerged, showing off God's handiwork. Every part of nature was a picture to behold.

Melinda searched for a soft place to lie down. She spied a beautiful patch of weeds that looked like spearmint or catnip, yet they were taller. She noticed the leaves were heart-shaped with ragged edges that tapered to a point at the end. It looked so inviting that she collapsed upon them.

The weeds were soft and comfortable beneath her. As she lay upon her soft bed of weeds, she leaned her face into them to smell the mint fragrance, but instead of smelling like mint, it bit her nose, cheeks, eyelids and mouth. Her hands and lower arms began to sting as if bees or mosquitoes were attacking her.

Melinda instantly jumped up and squealed in pain, looking for the insects that had attacked her, but she found none at all. Her face felt as if it were on fire and her hands and arms prickled with intense pain. The pain was unbearable and she ran home to Aunt Martha as fast as she could run.

When Martha saw the white raised blotches all over her face, she recognized it at once. "Stinging nettle," she exclaimed. "Melinda, what did you do? Lay down right in the middle of stinging nettle? You poor girl. Let me fix you up. Go upstairs and take off your clothes so I can wash them. I will be right up to take care of you, my poor dear. I'm so sorry. And your wedding is tomorrow. Oh my, what a sight you will be. Sometimes people itch for a few hours, but I itched for twenty-four hours straight because I have sensitive skin. I suspect that you will be the same, Melinda. Your skin is so fair and sensitive. You may be itching as you say the words 'I do' tomorrow."

Melinda was in pain as she walked upstairs to her bedroom. Tears began to well up in her eyes and her chest was heavy with emotion. As she looked in the mirror, she saw white itchy bumps all over her skin and her face was a sight. She groaned in despair as she rubbed her itchy arms. How could this happen to her on the eve of her wedding day, of all days? She began to sob as she looked at herself in the mirror. She just had to postpone it. There was no way she was going to look like this on the most important day of her life.

After undressing and putting on her cream-colored nightgown, she sat on the bed as Aunt Martha proceeded to rub a mixture of baking soda and water all over her skin to relieve the itching. "I wish I had witch hazel. It works well, but this will have to do. Melinda, this will soothe the itching but it won't make it go away. I'm sorry, dear."

After Martha finished, Melinda looked like a white splotchy mess. When she stood and looked in the mirror, she moaned. Her stomach twisted into knots and she told Martha, "You need to call on Gilbert. Tell him I'm putting off the wedding until next week."

"But Melinda, what if you get better tonight?"

"What if I don't? I can't cancel at the last minute. That wouldn't be fair to Gilbert."

Aunt Martha could see that Melinda would not listen to reason. She sighed, "All right, dear. I'll ride out to his place and explain to him."

When Martha returned home, Gilbert had come along with her on his horse. Martha led the way to Melinda's bedroom door and then left him to talk to her. Gilbert very gently knocked on her door.

"Melinda, it's me, Gilbert. May I come in and talk to you?"

Melinda gasped. "No, no. Go away, Gilbert. Please don't come in."

"But I need to talk to you."

"I can't let you in, Gilbert. I look terrible." Melinda began to cry and between sobs, she explained, "I'm ugly. I have white bumps all over my face and arms and hands. I have white goop all over me and I still itch." She took a shaky breath. "Please go away, Gilbert."

"But Melinda, I love you no matter what you look like. Please, let me come in so we can talk."

"Go away, Gilbert." This time her voice was firm.

"Melinda, I don't care what you look like. I'm in love with the Melinda that is inside of you. The outside doesn't matter. I would love you no matter what you looked like."

"Go away, Gilbert."

"Please, Melinda, let me come in."

"No, Gilbert. Go away."

Gilbert heard her burst into tears and begin to sob once again. He knew her stubborn personality and he knew that he could not coax her into doing something with which she was uncomfortable. But he was just as stubborn as she was and he would not leave. He knew she was weeping and he knew she was sad and depressed. Leaving her in this state of mind and in her misery was not what he wanted to do. He knew he must let her know in no uncertain terms that he had undying and unconditional love for her. But how?

Immediately he thought of Thomas Moore. "Melinda, I'm not leaving. I'm going downstairs and I'm coming right back."

Martha was in the kitchen when Gilbert entered. She looked at him with questioning eyes but Gilbert just asked her for a paper and ink and then he sat down at the table to write her a love note. As he wrote, he poured his heart out to her the best way he could. He did not feel that he was a very romantic person. He was not a Thomas Moore and he knew it, but he did the best he could. This time he would not compare her to a bull as he did at the terminal, but to a delicate flower.

A SPECIAL FLOWER

Flowers and friends are one and the same.
Each flower has a different scent,
Color, shape, and beauty of its own,
And so does each friendship in my life.
As I nurture and care for each flower,
My love for each friendship grows.
Each flower becomes a part of me
And I know that my life is happier.

But there is one special flower
That brings me great joy.
I love its color, shape, and scent.
This flower makes me smile.
This flower makes me laugh.
A friend, you may say?
No, you are much more than that.
You are this very special flower.

Then Gilbert wrote beneath his poem of love, "Melinda, the wish of my heart is to hold you in my arms and comfort you when you are sad, lonely, and depressed. May I have my wish?"

After folding the note, he marched upstairs and tapped at the door. Then he slid the note under her door. He watched as the edge of the note disappeared from sight. Then Gilbert waited and waited. He paced the hall back and forth. The minutes that followed seemed like hours, and still he waited. After a while, he began to think that he was going to have to ask for a pillow and blanket so he could stay overnight. He could not desert her at the lowest time of her life.

Then Gilbert heard footsteps approach the bedroom door and he turned toward the sound. His heart fluttered as he waited, wondering if she had softened and would allow him to talk to her. As he watched the door open slowly, Melinda stood in her cream-colored nightgown and robe with her eyelids lowered. Her dark auburn hair was brushed out and hanging gracefully about her shoulders and her face looked like a white blotchy mess. White patches were all over her face, neck, and hands, and she stood still as if she were ashamed. When she raised her eyelids, he could see that her eyes had a forlorn and unhappy look and he knew she felt embarrassed.

Gilbert's heart went out to her and he immediately enfolded her in his arms and said, "Oh, Melinda. How could you ever doubt my feelings for you? You're beautiful to me no matter what you look like."

Then all was silent except for a few sobs that were muffled by Gilbert's shoulder. Gilbert held her lovingly in his arms as he stroked her silky hair with his hand and tenderly rubbed her back. The feelings he had for this woman were deep. In fact, there seemed to be no words that could adequately describe his feelings for her.

As the wetness of her tears soaked through his shirt, he felt her anguish. "Oh, Melinda, I love you. You're the only woman meant for me. I know this. If I traveled across the universe searching for a mate, I wouldn't be satisfied with anyone but you." Then he realized that Melinda's happiness was more important to him than anything else. He could not coax her into marrying him when she felt so embarrassed. "Melinda, if you want to wait until next week to get married, I'll wait for you as long as it takes."

Gilbert held her tightly against his chest and snuggled his face into her neck. After a few seconds, he commented, "Hmmm, you smell like soda."

Gilbert pressed his lips against her neck and gave her a couple of tender kisses. "Mmm, you taste like soda."

Once again he sampled her neck a few more times, nibbling as he went, until Melinda began to squirm and giggle. Quickly, she pulled away from his arms and lifted her shoulder upward so she could protect her neck.

"Stop, Gilbert. That tickles."

"Melinda, I've got an idea," he said with a twinkle in his eyes and a mischievous grin. "How about if we mix cinnamon and sugar with the soda mixture and smear it all over your face and neck? Then I'll sample it to see how it tastes. Mmmm, what do you think?" Then he wiggled his eyebrows mischievously.

Melinda burst into a fit of laughter while Gilbert grinned from ear to ear. He began to chuckle in a low and pleasant voice as he watched her laugh.

Then she narrowed her eyes and asked, "Gilbert, are you trying to make me laugh?"

"Is it working?" He winked at her teasingly.

"Yes."

"Then in that case, I admit that I am."

"You mean to tell me that if I hadn't laughed, you would have denied it?"

"Probably so, Melinda. I hate to admit to failure."

Melinda burst into another fit of laughter as she wrapped her arms around Gilbert's chest and leaned her head against his shoulder. As she laughed, Gilbert wrapped his arms about her shoulders and chuckled deeply. He slid his fingers through her silky auburn hair and smiled. His plan had worked and she was happy once again.

When Aunt Martha came to the door of her room, she heard Melinda laughing softly and asked, "Well? What do you say, Melinda? You would disappoint more people than Gilbert if you cancel, you know."

Gilbert pulled back and looked into Melinda's eyes lovingly and said, "You know how I feel, Melinda. I hate to wait, but whatever you choose is all right with me. I don't want you to feel uncomfortable."

Melinda's heart was healed and she nodded her white blotchy head and sent Gilbert on his way. She would not put off their marriage after all.

The day of their wedding, Gilbert stood straight and tall and happiness filled his soul as he watched Melinda enter the room to be his wife for eternity. Even though he was six-feet-two inches tall, he felt taller that day.

Gilbert took her soft warm hand in his. As they looked at one another, Gilbert seemed to hold her eyes with his compelling gaze and the message he communicated was one of devotion and adoring love. Melinda still had small patches of white bumps on her face and hands, but she smiled at Gilbert as she said those magical words, "I do."

Author's Notes

Most of the classroom incidents throughout this novel were taken from true experiences of family members and ancestors. Jenny's experience with her former teacher when she was placed behind the bookshelves and the "saying" that her new teacher wrote on the board were taken from an actual experience. In reality, the teacher's daughter had written home, telling her mother of an inspirational talk she had heard by a church leader. He had said, "I love you even if you spit on me every day. I would love you more because you need it more" (Anonymous). The teacher, in turn, wrote the "saying" on the blackboard, hoping to inspire love and understanding among her students. It worked! The children giggled at the statement, but learned what she was trying to teach them. This experience stayed with me so powerfully that I included it in my novel.

Jenny's fishing experience and walking with pans tied to her feet were also taken from true experiences of my daughter, Felicia. Mark happened to be my father, Marcus

Gilbert Weaver, who had taken the skunk oil to school in the early 1920s. The school had to be abandoned for the day until it was aired out and he received no punishment afterwards.

The bank robbery incident by Butch Cassidy was a true experience that occurred in Montpelier, Idaho, in 1896, and is told by local Bear Lake Historian Pat Wilde in his book *Treasured Tidbits of Time, Volume 1*. I used every detail of the robbery in my novel to educate my readers about what the settlers had to put up with and about Cassidy's method of planning his robberies. Every year, Montpelier puts on a reenactment of the robbery for the public.

Of all the western outlaws, there seems to be a feeling of intrigue when the stories of Butch Cassidy and the Wild Bunch are told. Perhaps it is because many referred to him as the "Robin Hood of the West." He believed this and actually wrote, "The best way to hurt them is through their pocket book. They will holler louder than if you cut off both legs. I steal their money just to hear them holler. Then I pass it out among those who really need it." (Taken from *History of Butch Cassidy, LeRoy Parker,* from www.Utah.com.)

Robert LeRoy Parker, alias Butch Cassidy, was born April 15, 1866, in Beaver, Utah, and was raised by kind and religious parents. He worked on a ranch near Circleville, Utah. While a teenager, Parker became a good friend with an old rustler named Mike Cassidy. After Parker left home, he took on the name of his mentor. Cassidy was known for his quick wit, charm, fearlessness, and bravery, which made him a good leader of his gang and very likeable. Cassidy and his gang were known for the longest sequence of successful robberies in the history of the American West. As far as the historians know, he never killed a person in a robbery.

The Ice Palace was real and it was just as I described. People from all over the country traveled to the Ice Palace to see this magnificent sight. It melted in March of that same year, 1896.

There are several springs that come out of the Rocky Mountains in Cache Valley. When I was young, my father would take us to the Willow Flat Springs, not too far from Bear Lake Valley, and he would call it "The Source of the Nile." He made sure that we took cups with us so we could drink from the pure spring water that poured out of the mountain and I remember how delicious it was. When I took my sixteen-year-old daughter, Diana, to this source, there was a nest of white butterflies near the opening where the water was pouring out. When we sat down on a rock to watch them, she extended her finger and one butterfly after another alighted on her finger. She was so delighted and it was an experience that we never forgot.

There are numerous accounts of bear attacks in the Rocky Mountains. When I read a few autobiographical accounts of bear attacks in the 1800s and early 1900s that a few mountain men and an Idaho farmer had recorded, I discovered the fear that a person truly feels and I was amazed. The descriptions they used opened my eyes to such terror that I had never realized before. One mountain man said he actually shook for half an hour after he shot the grizzly that was charging after him. In my research, I found that to be approached by a grizzly is quite a terrifying experience.

This novel is one of four in the series, A Family Saga in the Bear Lake Valley: *Melinda and the Wild West, Edith and the Mysterious Stranger, Jenny's Dream,* and *David and the Bear Lake Monster.* Each story in this family saga has intrigue, excitement, and romance. Intertwining fact and fiction, these novels have a blend of intriguing characters and true experiences.

Acknowledgments

I give special thanks to my editor, Courtney Littler, who was invaluable to me and helped me in so many ways. Her point of view helped me a great deal. She is the best! And thanks to George A. Clarke for creating a lovely book cover. He has great talent. The picture that he used was from www.untraveledroad.com. I would like to give thanks to Kelvin Smith for the use of the beautiful photo. His photos are excellent.

About the Author

Linda Weaver Clarke was raised on a farm surrounded by the rolling hills of southern Idaho and has made her home in southern Utah among the beautiful red mountains and desert heat. She has been happily married for thirty-three years, is the mother of six daughters, and has four grandchildren.

Linda received her Bachelor of Arts degree in theater and music at Southern Utah University and received the Outstanding Non-traditional Student Award for the College of Performing Arts in 2002. She has been an active recitalist for the past eighteen years and cut a CD named *Romantic Love Songs of Sigmund Romberg and Victor Herbert*.

***

To learn more about this author or to schedule a speaking engagement, please visit www.lindaweaverclarke.com.